KRISTA'S CHANCE

GEMMA JACKSON

POOLBEG

Published 2020
by Poolbeg Press Ltd.
123 Grange Hill, Baldoyle,
Dublin 13, Ireland
Email: poolbeg@poolbeg.com

A catalogue record for this book is available from the British Library.

ISBN 978178199-3514

www.poolbeg.com

Also by Gemma Jackson

Through Streets Broad and Narrow

Ha'penny Chance

The Ha'penny Place

Ha'penny Schemes

Impossible Dream

Dare to Dream

Her Revolution

Published by Poolbeg

Foreword

Hello, dear Reader,

Welcome to *Krista's Chance*. So glad you have travelled along with me for the journey. How are you enjoying these shorter reads? I am loving getting them out to you in such quick time. Many of my readers have requested I write faster!

We join Krista as she is setting off on a camping trip. I was introduced to camping by my daughter, through sheer desperation. After yet another cold, damp, miserable summer in Ireland, I was determined to take off and chase the sun. I love Ireland. I love living here but, dear Lord, *I NEED THE SUN*. I kid you not. I often take off to chase it.

Before leaving Dublin, a long-time neighbour insisted on putting an old tent he had on hand in my car. I had never been camping in my life and didn't intend to start then – but he wouldn't take no for an answer. To keep the peace, I allowed him to put it in. The car was a sort of station wagon so the daughter and I had plenty of room. The tent had no stakes, my neighbour told me, which meant absolutely nothing to me. We took off for France.

I had intended to spend three days sleeping in the car then have a hotel stopover to shower and what not. Bad idea. Every hotel I could afford was fully booked. I drove around France, passing more and more signs with tents on them. I was determined to find a hotel room I could afford. Finally, in desperation, I followed my daughter's directions to the nearest camp site. It was becoming dangerous for me to keep driving.

My daughter unpacked the little tent. I found out what tent stakes are then – they are the things you stick in the ground to hold down the guy ropes. My daughter, an experienced camper, used knives, forks and spoons instead. We slept on the bare ground with towels under us and coats over us.

When the sun rose in the morning, I unzipped the tent's opening to look out onto a world of sheer beauty. We were right near the beach, almost falling into the sea. An older couple were stepping out of a campervan across from us. There was a beautiful domed tent to one side of it. I said over my shoulder to my grumbling daughter (she does not like mornings) how I thought it was a wonderful idea to bring along a tent for the grandchildren. The beautiful tent was opened and out jumped the dogs! The dogs had a prettier tent than we did.

I always carry tea-makings with me. I had a gas stove, kettle and all I needed for tea in the back of the car. I brewed up my first pot of tea. A lovely Frenchman approached me and asked if I would be offended if he offered me a table and chairs which I could use to break my fast!!! He didn't like to see us sitting on the grass.

When I went to pay the bill for the site, the ridiculously low cost astonished me. We left the tent in place and took off to tour the area in the car. When we returned to eat, I was once again offered the table and chairs. This time we were asked if we would be offended if another camper offered us a large salver of fresh seafood she had left over. Lobster, crab, shrimp. I wasn't in the least offended.

We packed up our tent the next morning, thanking our French campers profusely for their kindness. I set off for a shop I had noticed and bought everything I could possibly need to camp throughout Europe. I was hooked. I found out the French for tent stakes is *sardines* and I was all set. I have been pitching my tent around the world ever since.

Chapter 1

"You look delightful, my dear."

"Thank you, Captain Caulfield."

Krista waltzed to the delightful music of the orchestra in the arms of a handsome man in full-dress naval uniform. She smiled to think of the dance classes held at her school in France. There her partner was more often than not another girl. She always played the gent, being the tallest girl in her class.

"Charles, my dear," said the captain.

"I couldn't possibly!"

Krista was swept expertly across the magnificent ballroom. The light cast by the many glittering chandeliers caught the pearls in her hair, around her throat and the thin thread of silver in the white of her ballgown, making

1

her look like a glowing candle against the white of the captain's dress uniform. The medals and awards on his chest gleamed.

"You have no difficulty calling my wife 'Lia'," he said.

Charles had agreed to attend the ball at the Duke of Stowe-Grenville's country pile. It had taken a great deal of planning to arrive on time for this event. His ship was on manoeuvres off the coast of Scotland. He'd left his first officer in command. He would have to leave early Monday morning. His darling wife asked little of him. She had wanted him to escort her to this ball. How could he refuse? He smiled as his wife danced past in the arms of her brother Albert, Lord Winchester. She looked like a flame in her scarlet gown which hugged her body in a way that delighted his senses. The diamonds and rubies she wore at her neck and wrists caught the light.

"She looks like a film star this evening." Krista had followed the direction of his eyes. She ignored his request to call him Charles. She simply could not call this man – who looked like a picture-book hero – by his Christian name. "You are a very fortunate man."

"I am aware of my blessings." Charles smiled, thinking of the night ahead.

Time passed delightfully, with the group comprising Lord and Lady Winchester and their daughter Beatrice, Captain Caulfield, Lia and Krista meeting up to seek refreshment and compare notes on the evening, parting, dancing and generally enjoyed the lavish entertainment on offer. The orchestra ceased playing when the guests were called to dine.

"What fortunate men we are!" Albert, Lord Winchester, looking distinguished in white tie and tails, with his wife Abigail on one arm and his blushing daughter Beatrice on the other, prepared to walk into the dining room.

"We are the envy of all." Charles laughed, his wife Lia on one arm and Krista on the other.

The dining room glittered with a display of wealth that rendered Krista speechless. She tried to keep her eyes away from the fleet of servants, the gleam of silver, the glitter of crystal. She felt a fraud in her elegant gown, borrowed pearls in her hair, around her throat and on her wrists over her long evening gloves which perfectly matched the silvered white material of her gown. She did not belong here!

Krista was tired, her feet ached. She had danced, made polite conversation and smiled until her face hurt. It was the early hours of the morning. What time did something like this end? Was she the only one ready to leave?

"Excuse me, His Grace would like a word."

Krista turned from her conversation with the captain and Lia to see the commanding figure of the Duke's butler standing at her shoulder.

"I beg your pardon?"

"If you would follow me, madam. His Grace wishes a word with you."

"Certainly." Krista bowed her head graciously, desperately trying not to let the panic she felt show on her face.

"Krista, my dear," Abigail, Lady Winchester, feathers and jewels fluttering, appeared at her side as if by magic, "what is happening?" Her eyes demanded answers of the butler.

"His Grace desires a word with this young lady." The butler wasn't proof against the force of Abigail's silent demand.

"Does he indeed?" Abigail straightened her spine, ready to do battle.

Albert, Lord Winchester, knew that look. "My dear." He had to step in and stop his wife from giving everyone – looking out of the corner of their eyes at this unusual occurrence – a show.

"But, Bertie!" Abigail objected to the command in her husband's eyes.

"Abigail, we must step aside." Lia too was aware of the discreet interest of the crowd around them. They had been aware of the risk they had taken, bringing Krista into this house.

This was a family matter. They could not interfere.

"Who are you?" His Grace the Duke of Stowe-Grenville didn't turn when the butler closed the door to his study after announcing Krista. He stood with one arm braced on the fireplace mantel, a brandy goblet in hand, staring up at the large painting hanging on the chimney breast. He cut an impressive figure for his age. His evening attire of white tie and tails flattered his upright carriage. His silver hair was brushed back and oiled, revealing his harsh-featured face.

"A guest in your home, Your Grace." Krista kept her eyes on her feet.

"Don't bandy words with me, young woman – you are outgunned!" he barked, without sparing her a glance. He had seen all he needed to see as this young woman danced around his ballroom – her every gesture and movement was familiar to him. He turned slowly to look at her standing before him with eyes lowered, hands demurely clasped in front of the full skirts of her gown. "I asked you who you are – you will answer me."

"I have given you my answer, Your Grace." Krista raised her eyes to stare at the man she knew was her great-grandfather. "I am a guest in your home."

"Look at her!" He waved the hand not holding a glass towards the painting. "Look well at her and tell me again who you are."

"I am nobody, Your Grace." Krista stared at the portrait of an older woman. The features were familiar – she saw them every day in the mirror – the woman's silvering hair added to the resemblance.

"This family does not breed many females." The Duke thought of his lost granddaughter with familiar pain. He stared at the purity of the girl's face, raised to examine the portrait of his mother. "I want to know which of my sons or indeed my grandsons – as you appear quite young – *has dared to bring his by-blow into my home!*" He almost roared – heads would roll. Who among his progeny would dare such a thing? They were all financially dependent upon him. He wanted to know who had dared break society's rules in such a way.

"I am a French orphan, Your Grace, here at the invitation of friends who have welcomed me to this country." Krista refused to tell him what he wanted to know.

"You cannot so forcefully resemble my mother without being some relation to my family. I ask again, *who are you?*"

"I am tired, Your Grace." Krista's heart hurt. "I have enjoyed my time in your home." She turned towards the door. "I wish you goodnight."

"*I have not given you permission to withdraw.*" The Duke, a bastion of British nobility, could not believe this slip of a girl dared defy him.

"You and your family have given me nothing, Your Grace." Krista looked over her shoulder, her hand on the doorknob. "Goodbye." She stepped from the room and shut the door. She held her body upright with great difficulty. She longed to collapse back against the closed door and sob. She was shaking and wanted only to escape. She ignored the roar of demand that followed her.

"Krista, there you are!" Abigail appeared in the hallway. She had shaken off her husband and family, needing to be here for Krista. Her daughter Beatrice was surrounded by gossiping young girls, positively agog at the disappearance of Krista from the ballroom in the company of the Duke's butler. The foolish, foolish man – he was old enough to realise his every move was scrutinised.

"May we leave?" Krista wanted to leave this sprawling house, its every feature demonstrating the wealth and power of the family who called it home.

"Of course we can." Abigail wanted to cry at the emotional pain etched on the young face. She had no doubt she would be sent for in the coming days to answer questions from the Duke. She only hoped she wouldn't box his ears. The old goat!

***

The sound of swishing curtains being pulled back shocked Krista awake. She would never become accustomed to servants entering her room while she slept. She threw one arm over her eyes when harsh winter sunlight streamed through the lace curtain.

"Sorry, miss." The uniformed maid turned to the occupant of the bed. "M'lady said it was time you were up and about."

"What time is it?" Krista tried to focus her eyes, to see the clock on her bedside table. It had been past four o'clock when she sought her bed.

"It's gone eleven, miss." The maid stepped into the hall to retrieve the tray she had left on the hallstand outside the bedroom. She had needed her hands free to open the curtains.

"Eleven!" She had never slept so late in her life.

"Yes, miss." The maid carried the tray to the bed and waited. "If you would sit up, miss."

"Yes, of course," Krista felt wool-headed this morning. She pulled her aching body into a sitting position, bunching the pillows behind her back for support.

"Tea and toast, miss." The maid put the tray over Krista's lap. "Just the thing to set you up for the day." She turned to leave.

"Thank you!" Krista called after her swiftly departing figure.

"You are welcome, miss."

Krista poured tea into the delicate cup with a sigh. She would have preferred coffee. She needed something to wake her up fully. Dancing all night was a great deal more fatiguing than she would ever have imagined.

Thank goodness that would be the first and last time she would be called upon to do such a thing.

"Krista," the bedroom door was flung open, "you are such a slugabed! I declare I do not know how I have waited for you to awaken." Beatrice, eldest daughter of Lord and Lady Winchester, exploded into the room. She was dressed for the day in a stunning dress of green, every hair in place.

"Beatrice," Krista groaned, "how on earth can you be so full of energy. I am barely awake!"

"I did tell you to take a nap yesterday." Beatrice carried a chair over to the bed and, without asking permission, parked it and took a seat. "You ignored my good advice."

"So you did and so I did." Krista had never, to her knowledge, taken a nap in the middle of the day. When the ladies had all taken to their beds yesterday she had explored the grounds.

"Isn't this cherry preserve delightful?" Beatrice helped herself to a slice of toast from Krista's tray, spreading the jam thickly over a coating of yellow butter. "Cook makes it every year."

"Lovely." Krista pushed the plate of toast closer to her visitor. She could not eat upon awakening.

"Was not last evening the most wonderful evening you have ever known?" Beatrice asked around a mouth filled with bread and jam.

She reached for Krista's cup but she pulled it away from the reaching hand. She would share toast she did not want but drew the line at sharing a cup!

"Sorry," Beatrice giggled. "My sister and I shared food and drink all of the time, much to our governess's despair."

"Beatrice," Krista leaned back against the pillows, feeling old and tired, "you are a wonderful person – but has anyone ever told you that you are exhausting first thing in the morning?"

"Oh, everyone!"

Beatrice's delighted peals of laughter brought a reluctant smile to Krista's face. It was impossible to remain cross with the girl.

"Now!" Beatrice used Krista's napkin to wipe her face and hands. She picked up the milk jug from the tray and with no apology drank from it, her pale-blue eyes dancing over the rim of the china jug. "Tell me all."

"All?"

"Krista, do not be so mean. You were called to the Duke's private rooms. We all of us saw his butler lead you from the ballroom." Beatrice had a milk moustache. "Tell me all!"

"You have a moustache," Krista held up the napkin, waiting while Beatrice removed the milk stain. It gave her a brief moment to gather her thoughts. She needed to come up with a convincing story or Beatrice was quite capable of inventing one of her own.

"You are being excessively meanspirited." Beatrice sulked. "I want to know what the Duke of Stowe-Grenville wanted with you. Please," she begged, "tell me!"

"I am afraid there is not very much to tell." Krista lied without blinking. She could not afford to let Beatrice know of the secrets in her life. Beatrice was a delightful young lady, but she did love to gossip. "The Duke's butler made an error in judgement. I was not the young lady the Duke wished to speak with."

"*Nooo!*" Beatrice's face reflected her disappointment.

She had been sure she would have a delightful titbit of gossip to share with her many friends.

"Yes, it was a case of mistaken identity." Krista began to remove the tray from her lap. She needed to visit the bathroom. "I did not stay very long. The Duke was most displeased with his butler's error."

"Oh!" Beatrice, firmly lodged in her chair, was blocking Krista's escape.

"I need to use the bathroom." Krista pulled at the bedclothes.

The bedroom she had been given was set up with the bed pushed close to the wall on one side. This allowed the room to have a comfortable seating and reading area. There was also a desk and chair if one needed to write letters. It allowed one to escape from the other guests in the house if one felt the need. There was a narrow aisle on the far side of the bed from Beatrice. She supposed it was to allow the servants to dress the bed and dust. But you had to practically kiss the wall if you stepped from the bed on that side.

"Rather urgently, Beatrice."

"Yes, of course." Beatrice wasn't listening, the picture of dejection.

"You need to move the chair, please."

The door to the bedroom opened.

"Krista, there was a telephone call for you." Lia, dressed for the day, walked into the room. "Beatrice, I did not know you were here."

"Aunt Lia." Beatrice settled into the chair with a smile. Now she would hear something interesting, she had no doubt.

"Ladies, please," Krista was becoming desperate. "I

need to use the toilet or I am about to disgrace myself."
She pushed back the bedclothes and, avoiding the tray,
crawled to the foot of the bed to make her escape.

Chapter 2

Krista stepped back into her bedroom, much refreshed. She cast her eyes around, looking for Beatrice.

"It is safe to return," Lia said with a laugh. "Beatrice too received a telephone call. It was from one of her many young friends – Tuffy or Muffy or some such silly person. She has dashed away to return the call."

Lia guessed that Beatrice had been trying to ferret out information about the previous evening from Krista. She herself had not asked Krista about her meeting with the Duke of Stowe-Grenville. It had been obvious from the strain on the girl's face, when she returned to the ballroom with Abigail, that matters had not gone well. If Krista wanted to tell her she would, of course, listen. Until then the matter was best left alone.

"She is a delightful young woman." Krista closed the door at her back with relief. She passed no further comment. After all, Beatrice was the daughter of Lia's brother.

"But exhausting and too fond of gossip." Lia knew her niece well. "You never thought to use Beatrice as a model for the sort of bright young thing Captain Waters wanted you to mimic?"

"I would not be capable of keeping up that level of energy." Krista didn't say that the very thought of acting in a manner similar to Beatrice's gave her a headache. She had been asked to participate in an operation for the British government. It would be necessary for her to present herself as a member of the ruling classes. She had worked long and hard on the image she needed to present.

"Captain Waters telephoned this morning," Lia said, lowering her voice, and walked over to the window away from the door.

The Louis Vuitton suitcases she had purchased for Krista to use were sitting empty on the desktop and tabletop as she had instructed. She did not want the servants to take the luggage to the attics or storage rooms. The news from the Continent was dire. She had feared the items of luggage might be needed at a moment's notice. She had instructed Krista to study the luggage carefully. She must know every zipper and pocket. They were items she would have to handle with familiarity should the need ever arise. In point of fact, she had almost driven herself insane trying to think of every eventuality.

"I took the liberty of responding to the telephone

call for you." She turned to look at Krista with a smile. "You needed your beauty sleep."

"Thank you. Does he want me to return his call?" Krista joined Lia in front of the closed window.

"There was no need." Lia was worried about Krista. The mission she had accepted could be deadly. "He gave me your instructions."

They both spoke in low tones.

"Do you not mean orders?" Krista prompted when Lia remained silent. Graham Waters expected one to jump when he spoke.

"Yes, of course I do." Lia shook off her worry. The die was cast. "He will pick you up from here tomorrow morning. You are to wear the outfit we have chosen for you to travel in." Lia had been instructed to choose clothing to suit the role that Krista was about to play. She had spent days touring the modiste shops in and around London. She was pleased with the selections she had made. It was to be hoped that she had covered every eventuality.

The day before the ball the two women spent hours in the room set aside for Krista's use. Krista had tried on all of the items Lia had selected. She had listened to her advice about forming separate items into attractive outfits. The evening gown Lia selected for Krista to wear to the Duke's ball had been a triumph.

"I will summon a servant and oversee your packing while you dress," Lia said.

"Lia, wait – I appreciate everything you have done for me – more than I can ever express. But you need to go away." She laughed at the look of surprise on Lia's face. "You spend so little time with your husband. Go spend time with your family. We have covered everything I need to know about the image I must present. The maid can assist me with my packing." She pushed Lia gently in the direction of the door. "Go, have fun with your handsome husband and your children. I will be absolutely fine."

"You will take care." Lia dug her heels in to stop Krista practically forcing her from the room.

"I promise." Krista accepted the tight hug from Lia before she resumed pushing her towards the door. "Go, spend as much time as you can with your husband. I know he has to return to his ship."

"You will join the family for lunch?"

"Of course." Krista was hungry. She would be ready for a meal by the time she had dressed for the day. "I want to say goodbye to David and Edward."

"The twins will miss you." Lia laughed. "They have become accustomed to their little outings with you. I do not know if I can live up to your example."

"They have their schoolfriends now." Krista would miss the twins but she would see them again. "I will join you for lunch and be in the driveway waving you and your family off. I promise."

The two women parted company, Lia fighting tears. She was so desperately worried about the role Krista had agreed to play. She had done all she could to help. She prayed it was enough.

The following morning, after taking breakfast with the family, Krista stood before the long mirror set into the door of the wardrobe in her bedroom. She stared into the mirror at the image of the stranger she had become.

15

To her eyes she no longer bore any resemblance to the Krista who had worked every day in the bar/café/tabac of the *auberge de ville* in Metz, France. She frowned at the image, wondering what was in store for this version of herself.

The navy slacks she wore were far different from the pair she had purchased for herself. This pair were fully lined, the satin lining cool against her bare legs. The material was cashmere and hung in a very flattering fashion. The white silk blouse she wore under a navy cashmere jumper felt wonderful against her skin. She had tied the bow of the blouse just as Lia had taught her. She pulled up one leg of the slacks to admire her custom-made, navy, laced walking shoes. The leather felt as soft as butter. She felt she could run miles wearing these shoes. Even her stockings were of a vastly superior quality to anything she had ever worn before.

The ball gown and the clothes she had worn to travel to this house were stored, carefully packed in mothballs by a servant, in the vast attics.

"I wonder what Peggy and Mrs Acers would make of me now." Krista laughed to think of Lia's household servants. Peggy had thought Krista's wardrobe vastly superior to anything she could afford and had envied her. How would she feel if she could see this new expensive attire?

The Louis Vuitton suitcases, expertly packed by a maid, were sitting on the floor at her feet. She took a deep breath and saluted the image in the mirror. Now for the outer garments. The hip-length cherry-red swing coat made a statement, she felt. She put it on, leaving it open over her outfit for the moment. The cheeky Robin

Hood hat, dyed to match the coat, had a tall feather in its band. She put it carefully over her gleaming hair and stood for a moment to admire the woman in the mirror.

"They say that clothes maketh the man," She laughed softly. "Well, in my humble opinion, these clothes make me into a very different woman than the one I am accustomed to seeing. Yes, indeed, Krista Lestrange of no family name. You have come a long way in a short time." She stood for a moment, gearing herself up mentally for what was to come. She pulled the bell to summon a servant to carry down the luggage. She looked around the room, doing a final visual check before stepping into the corridor and pulling the door closed behind her.

Captain Waters would be here soon.

Chapter 3

Krista was surprised to be picked up by Captain Waters wearing his off-duty clothes and driving what she thought must be his own vehicle. He was unusually grim and refused to step into the house to greet the family. He wasted no time loading Krista's luggage and driving them from the Winchester estate out onto the main road in the direction of the coast. She tried to start a conversation but sat back in her seat to enjoy the journey when he only grunted in reply to her comments.

"We have arrived."

Krista started at his sudden announcement. She shook herself from her thoughts and looked around. The area was remote, an artery of a main road, she thought. The captain was pulling his car over onto the forecourt of a garage. There was a single petrol pump she imagined would serve farmers and passing salesmen.

"There you are, Evans – have you completed the work on her?"

A man, his oil-stained overalls proclaiming his profession, pulled a flat cap from his head and gave the captain a gap-toothed grin.

"Have I ever failed you, captain?" he said cheerfully.

He pulled open the double doors of his work area. The campervan was revealed when the light entered the large building. He patted its side lovingly.

"This little beauty has a lot of power under the hood. Who is going to drive her – not yourself?"

Krista stepped out of the captain's car.

"That will be my pleasure," she said, replacing the hat she'd removed in the car. The feather had been in danger of damage.

The captain did not introduce them.

Evans stared at the girl. She'd never be strong enough to manage the campervan surely? "If that don't beat all," he contented himself with saying. His old captain knew what he was about.

"Krista, we will load your luggage while we wait for Perry to join us. He should be along soon." Captain Waters began to remove Krista's luggage from his car and set it on the cement of the forecourt. "There have been some changes made to the interior." When he had the luggage stashed in the space underneath the vehicle, he said, "Step inside and I'll show you after I have had a word with Evans."

Krista stepped up into the campervan. She removed

her coat and hat, hanging the coat in the narrow wardrobe to one side of the bathroom. She put her hat on the shelf of the wardrobe before looking around. She noticed that the passenger seat beside the driver's had been removed. In its place was a wheelchair. She bent to examine the leather chair with its overlarge wheels and discovered it had been clamped in place with the same easy lock-and-release mechanism of the driver's seat.

"I think that is to be my chariot," Perry said as he stepped up into the van.

"Why?" Krista turned from where she had been crouched examining the mechanism on the chair.

"No 'Hello, Perry, wonderful to see you'?" He smiled to see her. He could not think of anyone he would rather have at his side on this little adventure.

"Hello, Perry," Krista parroted back to him, "wonderful to see you. How did you get here?"

"My mother's chauffeur drove me." He squatted beside her to examine the chair. "This is rather clever … But what is that doing there?" He pointed to an ornate urn placed on the floor between the wheelchair and the driver's seat.

"Your attention, please." Captain Waters, several file folders under one arm, stepped into the van.

He turned the driver's seat around to face the interior and threw the files on its seat. Then, with Krista's help, he took the table from its storage place and unfolded it in the centre of the floorspace. He placed the files on it.

"Sit," he said.

He sounded so grim that they immediately obeyed, taking the seat under the window.

He indicated the folders. "These contain all of the paperwork you'll need on your journey." He stared at the pair in front of him. They were so young. "The plan has changed," he said.

"What has happened?" Perry asked.

"News from Germany is of worsening tensions. Meanwhile, one factor in the operation has changed and increased the risk considerably. The basic plan, however, remains the same. You will travel into Germany, giving the appearance of a newly married couple, your mission being to smuggle out a person who is under threat."

A person? Was it not a couple – a scientist and his wife? Krista was about to ask when he continued.

"We want you to sail from Felixstowe to Antwerp in Belgium. From there you will directly drive across the nearby border and into Germany." He removed a map from one of his folders and spread it open over the table. When they stood to join him, he began to trace the route he wanted them to take on the map. "I will not mark the map as you will be taking it with you."

"When do we leave?" Perry asked.

"Immediately. You will camp overnight in a field near to the harbour in Felixstowe. It is imperative that you appear familiar with every feature of the van. If you should be stopped by officials and questioned, you must not falter in your answers. Perry has been shown all of the van's features and can instruct you, Krista."

Krista felt a fluttering in her stomach. Silly of her but she had given no thought to the close proximity of an attractive man in such close quarters. She had been worried about everything but that! She trusted Perry to behave as a gentleman but still …

"You two and the van are booked to take the ferry tomorrow. Your tickets, your passport and papers, showing you as a newly married couple called Carter, are in this folder. There are also traveller's cheques in different denominations to an amount that should cover all of your needs." Waters threw another folder on the table. "I trust you both not to be spendthrifts."

"No, sir," they answered together.

"I'll take care of the papers." Perry kept his head down to conceal his reddening cheeks. He had sisters but he had never lived in such close quarters with a female. He would behave himself – of course he would – he was not an animal. But still …

"Are we no longer required to amass intelligence?" Krista was being paid to accompany Perry on this mission because of her knowledge of languages and her, to English eyes anyway, Germanic looks.

"We will need every atom of intelligence you can gather. Now more than ever, but the situation has changed since this mission was originally planned." He had been warning the powers that be that Germany was dangerous to its neighbours for what felt like years. He had planned this information-gathering mission when he had thought there was still time. It would now appear they had run out of time.

"Captain, you just now spoke of 'a person' we must smuggle out," said Krista. "But it's a couple, isn't it? A scientist and his wife?"

"It will not now be a couple." Waters almost collapsed into the driver's seat. He took a deep breath through his nose. When he was sure he had control of his emotions, he continued. "The couple's children have been safely removed. The two youngsters are aboard a train full of children headed towards England and safety. The scientist …" he stopped and pinched the bridge of his nose, "has agreed to work for the Nazis. The mother is on the run in fear for her life. She plans to drive the family car until it runs out of petrol. She hopes to reach a remote train station where she will make her way by train and on foot to Essen. She is the one you *must* remove from Germany."

"So where will we meet her?" Perry asked. "And how will we recognise her? Should we not have a safe password?"

"You will stop and camp for two nights each in four rural areas inside Germany. The sites chosen are in close proximity to industrial sites. We want you to keep your eyes and ears open." He pointed to the ornate urn prominently displayed on the floor of the van between the driver's seat and the wheelchair. "Should you be questioned by officials at any time your cover story is this." He tapped the urn with a slight grimace. "This urn contains human remains."

"I misheard, I think?" Perry stared wide-eyed at Krista.

"The story you will give to anyone who asks –" Waters prayed it would never happen but in today's climate in Germany no one was safe, "is that the ashes belong to Krista's maternal great-grandmother – a German. You are fulfilling a promise Krista made to that woman on her deathbed. A promise to scatter her ashes in her favourite locations over the fields of her beloved Germany."

"Who do the ashes belong to?" Krista asked.

"A woman destined for a pauper's grave," Waters said. "She agreed, while dying, to allow us to use her ashes. She just asked that we set up a bench with her name engraved on a plaque on the grounds of her local church."

"Could you not have paid for a resting place for the poor woman?" Perry asked.

"I did what she asked of me." Waters almost laughed, thinking of the feisty old woman Evans had introduced him to. "She wanted to make people in her village think about how much money she might have had when they saw the fancy bench with her name on it." He did laugh now, surprised that he could. It was the old woman's joke on a world that had largely ignored her.

"If that was her wish." Krista thought of the portrait of her great-great-grandmother hanging in pride of place in her son's study. She would use the memory of that woman if anyone asked questions of her.

"The industries near to your camping sites have good train service which is of vital importance if this woman is to reach you. You must stop at all four places. It is imperative. I have given the woman all four locations. It is hoped if she can't make one, she will have a chance of joining you at another." Waters stopped.

"Captain, this all sounds very impractical." Krista couldn't imagine a woman on the run travelling across Germany. The trains were patrolled by soldiers. She would be checked frequently for her papers and reason for travelling through Germany. How would she answer?

"Krista, Perry," Waters stared from one to the other, "when this mission was planned we thought it would be prudent to remove the scientist from Germany but we did not feel that we were putting you in great danger. That is no longer the case." He took a deep breath. "We doubt that the German scientist will keep our original plan to himself. Possibly he will. For his wife's sake. But that remains to be seen." Thank God he had never told them he was about to send a young couple in a campervan to meet them.

"Captain, how have you been communicating with this couple?" Krista wanted to know.

"Carrier pigeon." He almost laughed at the surprise on both faces. "They will be an invaluable source of gathering information in the coming days. If I could, I would send a crate of the birds with you in the van!"

"Let me see if I understand." Perry was confused. "You want us to camp in four marked locations. We are to help an unknown female who may or may not join us to cross borders into England?"

"That is the mission." Captain Graham Waters knew it was a dangerous plan, but it must work – it simply must.

"How will we know if the woman showing herself to us is really the wife of this missing scientist?" Krista asked. "We know that Nazi soldiers can extract information from unwilling people. It would be a simple matter to send a woman to us, claiming to be the scientist's wife. We will have no way of knowing."

"Krista, Perry, the woman fleeing for her life through Germany is my twin sister." Graham Waters looked at them both. "We are so much alike that it would be impossible for anyone to fool you. Gisele is my female counterpart."

He laid a photograph on the table.

"Here she is."

"Good God!" Perry exclaimed.

"Oh, captain!" Krista shook her head.

Chapter 4

"Have you ever sailed, Krista?"

"No," Krista replied, her eyes firmly on the road. She wanted to laugh aloud at the very idea. She'd had little opportunity for adventure growing up. The walls of the *auberge de ville* had been her whole world, it sometimes seemed to her. "Why do you ask?"

"When I was being shown what was what in the campervan, it struck me as very similar to the small yachts I have sailed." Perry too was watching the road. He was keeping an eye on his driver too. He had been assured Krista had passed her driving test with distinction but his life was now in her hands. Not a comfortable position for him to find himself in.

"How so?" She was aware of his feet moving towards

non-existent controls on the floor at his feet. He was nervous about her driving!

"There is a place for everything," he replied. "It is a clever little craft with everything we might need for our comfort. However, we must return everything to its place and be sure it is locked down before we move the van."

"You will need to teach me and remind me until it becomes automatic to me." Krista didn't want to make mistakes.

"Yes." Perry wondered if he should mention something. With his fingers crossed that she would not take offence, he said, "I noticed you left the tea-makings out on the counter that time you made us a pot of tea, the first time we saw the van."

"This is all new to me, Perry." Krista was thankful one of them knew what they were about. "I will learn with your help."

"Are you nervous?" Perry asked after there had been silence for some miles.

"Very much so," Krista replied. They needed to be truthful with each other. From this moment on, they had only each other to depend on.

"Why?"

"I cannot like the fact that Captain Waters is so emotionally involved in the safe escape of the woman we are to meet. It is my opinion only, Perry, but did you not think he was making errors in judgement?"

"How so?"

"Why has he installed that chair?" She answered his question with her own, pointing to the wheelchair.

"He wishes me to exaggerate my infirmity." Perry had been in intensive French and German language lessons for this journey. He had also been receiving lessons in what the boffins were calling spy craft. He had been trained to take notice of everything around him, no matter how seemingly innocent. "It is believed that my infirmity will assure any officials who might question us of my ..." he stopped for a moment to think of how to phrase it, "uselessness," he finally said with slight bitterness.

"It is a mistake." Krista was frowning as she watched for the turn-off the captain had told them about. They were to camp in a farmer's field. With that man's permission. She thought it fortunate that they were to stop in an area that appeared deserted. It would give them a chance to discuss their mission. And she was nervous about this first night together. It was important that they set up rules and find a way to live together in such close quarters.

Soon the van was rattling over tractor tracks in the muck of the laneway she turned into.

"This is it." Perry's voice came out shakily as they came to a gate in a long white fence, leading into an empty green field.

She stopped the van and he stepped out, slamming the door behind him. "I'll close the gate after you," he said, speaking to her through the open window. "I suggest you park the van near that stream over there." He gave the side of the van a brief pat before going to open the gate.

Krista pushed herself up in the driver's seat, looking for the stream he'd mentioned. She saw it. She was biting her lip in concentration as she drove the van through the gate and over the field in its direction. She pulled up in what she considered a good spot and, with a sigh of relief, turned off the engine.

"Well done!"

Perry's voice caused her to jump. She hadn't been aware of him approaching.

"Let's get ourselves organised. We can have a cup of tea in the fresh air."

"Fresh air?" Krista questioned, stepping out of the van. "That wind would skin you."

"Serves you right for dressing as if you were going on a cruise!" He laughed at her shivers.

"What is wrong with what I'm wearing?" Krista held her hands away from her body. "This is the sort of outfit Captain Waters demanded."

"It would be wonderful if we were strolling along the deck of a cruise liner!" Perry opened the door into the shell of the campervan. "Go on, make us a pot of tea – I'll join you in a moment."

Krista took the spirit stove and stand out and put them on the counter that divided the top and bottom of the fitted cupboard.

"*In the name of God!*" came in loud tones from outside while the van shook.

She looked towards the door, wondering what was happening. Did he need help? She would busy herself with making tea and wait until he asked.

"Is all of that Louis Vuitton luggage stuffed into storage belonging to you?" Perry demanded in tones of shock.

"Who else would it belong to?" Krista snapped. After all, she was just doing what she was told.

"Thank you, Mother!" Perry, carrying two haversacks, raised his eyes to heaven as he stepped up into the van.

"Thank her for what? What has your mother to do with anything?"

"To do with anything?" Perry laughed out loud. "Imagine my amazement," he said as he dropped one of the haversacks on the floor, the other on the bench under the window, "when one of my instructors in covert operations turned out to be my own dear mother!" He had almost fallen out of his chair when she walked into the classroom and up to the lecturer's table. The woman who had kissed his hurts and held his hand through childhood – an expert in covert operations – it was a ground-shaking discovery for her son.

"You didn't know?" Krista didn't know why she was so surprised. After all, it seemed every day since she had arrived in England she discovered something she hadn't known about herself. Why should Perry be any different?

"I didn't have a clue." Perhaps he should have had when his father briefly mentioned his mother's brilliance. But what son could think of his own mother as a femme fatale?

"So what are you thanking her for?" Krista busied herself with making tea, waiting to hear what expert advice his mother had shared with him.

"Mother was of the opinion that a man should never be put in charge of a lady's wardrobe." Perry played with the ties on one of the haversacks. "Under any circumstances."

"Yes?" she prompted while moving a haversack and getting the table out.

"The clothes you are wearing, Krista, while delightful, are not suitable for camping in muddy fields."

"You are wearing a suit." A very expensive suit if she were any judge.

"Yes, I am, and I am about to change out of it and put it into storage for the duration of our journey."

"Oh, I see." She put mugs on the table with a glass bottle of milk she'd found in the cool box. This was no place for fine dining. She knew Perry like herself did not take sugar in his tea.

"Mother got your measurements from Captain Waters." Perry pointed to the haversack on the floor. "In there you will find oiled twill trousers, a mariner's jumper with leather elbows and an oiled soft hat to protect your face and hair. It also contains wellington boots and an oiled trench coat."

"*What?* After all the fuss that has been made about getting my wardrobe right? All the instructions delivered to Lia? All my dressing up and parading around? Now it turns out to be a waste of time?" Krista stood, hands on hips, furious.

"Calm down! Your fancy clothes may need to be aired yet – just not in a muddy field!"

Krista turned the driver's seat around and locked it into place then picked up her mug and sat down. She began to sip her tea, glad of the warmth.

"It is fortunate Captain Waters ordered us to camp here tonight," she said at last "We will have a chance to talk and exchange ideas and concerns."

"Yes, indeed." Perry sipped his tea, looking around at the space which suddenly seemed so much smaller to him. "We will be travelling in very intimate circumstances. The campervan does have a pull-out attachment outside which can be used for sleeping or dining but," he held up his hand when she looked to be about to speak, "we are into the month of November. It will be no weather for sleeping outside. In any case, we are supposed to be newlyweds so must give the impression of sleeping together. We will have to arrange ourselves as best we can inside the van at night."

"We will probably be glad to share body heat – I mean, of course, to share the same air." Krista tried not to blush. "The van is quite chilly."

"We do have a log fire," Perry said. "We will have to be sure to have logs and firing to hand when we travel."

The two sat for a while enjoying the pot of tea and thinking about the problems ahead.

"Krista," Perry said suddenly. "You never did tell me why you were so concerned at the introduction of the wheelchair into the van."

"I think it would be a grave error to present yourself as someone who has difficulties in getting around." She shivered as memory bit.

"You have a reason for saying that," Perry said. "From the look on your face it is far more than a woman's intuition."

Krista hesitated. She had to be careful in what she said. Perry had no idea she had grown up as the child of *auberge* owners, that she had worked in the family bar/café/tabac almost from the time she could toddle. She had no wish for a man she was going to travel in close confines with to suddenly think of her as a serving wench! "I am remembering conversations I overheard while living in France." She thought for a moment how best to explain her concerns. "I don't know quite how to explain. I overheard a great many things I did not understand. Conversations between men that meant next to nothing to me at the time." She shrugged. "Since

I arrived in England, I have been giving some consideration to those titbits of conversation. They now make more sense to me."

"And?" Perry prompted.

"In Germany today . . ." She jumped to her feet, wanting to pace but unable because of the small space. She gave a hastily suppressed groan of exasperation and sat back down. "Listen, I simply believe the last thing in the world you want to do is present yourself as handicapped in any way." She gulped air for a moment.

"Explain." It had been suggested to him that he exaggerate his injury and conceal his own physical fitness and capabilities. It was thought that a man with one leg impaired would not be considered a worry or a worthy opponent in any difficult situations that might arise.

"Not to put too fine a point on it," Krista was having difficulty even saying the words, "the men I overheard in conversation discussed the idea current in Germany of eliminating anyone who is not a perfect physical or mental specimen."

"Strange, I had heard something similar." Perry wanted to kick his own backside. Why had he not considered that he might be putting himself and Krista into a great deal of danger by playing such a role. What had any of them been thinking of? Perhaps it was simply because the thought of killing people who were not perfect was against everything a civilised people believed in?

"I think, Perry," Krista said slowly, "that from this point forward we should plan our own movements. We will, of course, gather as much information as we can. We will make every effort to meet up with the captain's sister … but Perry …" She paused to stare into his eyes. "We are on our own. We only have each other to count on. We must work as a team. If one of us has concerns, there can be no keeping them to oneself. We must discuss everything we think and do – together. Do you agree?"

"I agree." Perry nodded. "We will make every effort to work as a team and give our all to completing this mission and returning home."

They each reached out without thought and shook hands on the matter with slightly shamefaced smiles.

"Now," Perry slapped the top of the table, "if you will tidy away our equipment, I will change my clothing before stepping outside to use the bushes to relieve my needs. You may use the bathroom in the van."

"Where will you change?" Krista looked around the small space.

"We will start as we mean to go on with an honour system in place." Perry removed his suit jacket and hung it in the wardrobe alongside Krista's coat. "I will not look in your direction while you change. You will give me the same courtesy. Does that suit?" He was removing his shirt as he spoke.

"I believe I would prefer to sit with my eyes covered until you are finished." Krista sat in the driver's seat and covered her eyes with both hands.

"As you please." Perry opened his haversack and hunted out the outfit he planned to wear most frequently on their travels. He laughed softly to see Krista sitting with her hands almost clamped over her eyes as he continued to undress.

It seemed to Krista that many minutes has passed before she heard his voice again.

"You can look now." She heard him open the van door. "I shan't be long," He stepped outside laughing.

"Oh, dear Lord!" How on earth were they going to manage to live at close quarters like this?

She jumped to her feet and with haste restored order to the van, folding the table away. She almost ran into the tiny bathroom. There was a sort of toilet stand but it opened down directly onto the grass below. Heaven help her.

She was just stepping out of the bathroom when Perry returned.

"You should change. But now that the table is out of the way I can show you this. There is a concealing curtain that pulls along over the driver and passenger seats and allows us some small privacy. It is supposed to be used for sleeping but we can also use it while one of us washes and dresses."

"Fine." Krista was thankful for small mercies.

Perry withdrew behind the curtain.

Krista bent to open the haversack. "Oh – what is this?" She had pulled a strange-looking garment from the top of the haversack Perry's mother had prepared for her.

"May I look?" Perry's voice came from behind the curtain he had pulled across.

"You will have to!" Krista snapped. "I have no idea what this is." She shook the garment she held as soon as his head appeared around the curtain.

"You are holding the bottom half of the garments you will wear under your clothing."

"I beg your pardon?"

He laughed – the dog!

"There are several pairs of gents' undergarments included with the clothing my mother thought we both would need on this journey." Perry pulled the curtain back and stood up. It was obvious she was not going to dress until he explained further.

"Krista, we are both cold at this moment. It will be even colder on the ferry across the channel. We need clothing that will keep us warm. We cannot afford for either of us to fall ill."

"But these!" She shook the garment again. It was even uglier than her hated black woollen stockings!

"No one will see you wearing them, for goodness' sake!" Perry tried hard not to laugh at the look of outrage on her face. "They were designed for men undertaking long journeys in cold weather. I believe the American cowboys found them very useful."

"I am not a cowboy."

"Obviously not." Perry gave in and laughed until his sides ached. When he had sobered up, he put an arm around her shoulders. "Look," he bent at the waist, pulling her with him to look through the window at the side of the van. "We are in the middle of nowhere. We must learn how best to survive the coming weeks. We have no laundry facilities. The water we carry on board will be used sparingly unless we are parked near a stream. The type of garments my mother sent for you were used by men setting out across hostile environments. Please put them on." He squeezed her shoulders gently, pulling her upright. "If you find they do not work for you we will think of something else."

"Oh, very well." Krista was shivering. It was so cold, now that the engine had been turned off.

"I will light the fire. We need to warm this van up or we will never sleep."

Krista felt such a failure. Their very first night and she was close to tears. She wanted to kick the bench close to her.

"Perry? Do you know why Captain Waters insisted we travel in this fashion?"

"It is such a clever little craft." Perry had opened the cast-iron door of the little stove set snugly into its high iron fireplace surround. The cast-iron chimneystack travelled up and out of the top of the van. It would heat the van in no time. He was stuffing paper and kindling, kept in a locked box tucked into one side of the fireplace, into the stove. Really, there was a place for everything they could need. He put a match to the kindling and turned to look over his shoulder at his despondent companion. "This little beauty has everything we could need."

"That does not answer my question." Krista wanted to kick Perry now. How dare he be so cheerful!

"Captain Waters had this van designed with smuggling goods and people in mind. There are hidden compartments and moving walls that can be put into use if necessary. We are the first to use it." He'd been given instruction in concealing cargo of all shapes and sizes from all eyes. He took several logs from the box and put them on the now blazing kindling. He closed the door, dusted his hands and stood. "I cannot leave the door open. The van would fill with smoke, but we will soon feel the benefit of the fire."

"We are supposed to sleep, eat, bathe and smuggle people in this little thing?" Krista threw her arms wide. "It cannot be done."

"Yes, it can," Perry insisted. "You will see as we go along." He put his hands on her shoulders and gave her a gentle shake. "You are cold and tired. You need to change into warmer clothing. We will have something to eat while the van warms up."

He sat back down in the driver's seat and pulled the curtain across. He knew they were asking a great deal of Krista. He believed she was more than capable. She was simply overwhelmed at the moment. The noise coming from behind the curtain told him she was changing. He tried very hard not to think about what that meant.

Krista had a white-knuckled grip on the wheel as they prepared to drive away from the field the next morning. The gold ring she'd put on that morning gleamed on the third finger of her left hand. She was wearing the gent's winter undergarments and the oiled slacks and jumper. They felt strange on her body but Perry had assured her the heat of her body would cause the garments to settle around her. They were to head to Felixstowe docks. What a night! She felt as if her body was still blushing. There had been so many intimate matters they needed to discuss! Perry had been all that was gentlemanly but … he had to explain her very clothing to her! They had slept in bags for goodness' sake!

"I want you to drive very slowly towards the entrance to the field." Perry's voice came from the back of the campervan.

"Are you not going to sit down first?" She turned to look into the van.

"I want to look and listen as we leave." Perry was making a final check of the van interior. "I believe we have everything cleaned away and locked down, but I will not be sure until the van is moving."

"Hold tight!" Krista turned the engine on and began to drive very slowly towards the gate.

"I believe I will call the lady in the urn Brunhilda Alvensleben," Krista said as they drove towards Felixstowe.

"That is quite the name – why?"

Krista did not take her eyes from the road. "It is all very well for Captain Waters to tell us that the ashes are those of my great-grandmother but we will need more of a story than that if anyone should ask." She shrugged. "It is best to be prepared."

"I agree, so tell me about her." Perry was proud of Krista for the way she had behaved when faced with a situation that was difficult for both of them. They had spent a comfortable night, thanks to her willingness to obey his instructions.

"The urn is that of my great-great-grandmother, I have decided." Thinking about the lady in the urn had given her something to get her mind off the strangeness of spending a night in a van, in a field, with a man not her husband. "Her name of birth as I have said was Brunhilda Alvensleben. She lived to a great age, one hundred and three …"

"That is old. You might be stretching it a bit." Perry objected.

"We don't want anyone who might ask about the urn to claim they know someone old enough to remember her, now do we?"

"That danger had not occurred to me." Perry said. "Nor to Captain Waters it would appear."

"I have given a great deal of thought to my dear old grandmother – my *grosmutti*. I resemble her greatly, don't you know? Why, I was her very favourite grandchild." Krista laughed. It was nice to have a relative she could talk about!

They continued to make up outrageous stories about the bold Brunhilda as they drove on to Felixstowe

"I am so glad your mother insisted on kitting me out." Krista was standing on the deck of the ferry.

The campervan had been hoisted onboard. They were under way. The only part of her body feeling the biting cold of the whistling wind was her face. Every other inch was covered.

"I believe there is an area set aside on the deck below for passengers." Perry too was glad of his oiled outer garments. "Do you want to sit in out of this wind?"

"We will have to speak with our fellow passengers."

"It will be good exercise for us." Perry was nervous too. They had talked about the image they would present but this would be their first actual time of testing their story on strangers. "I had thought there would be more cars and people travelling."

"It is my firm opinion that no one in their right mind would travel in the first days of November," Krista said. "I would think in December people would travel for the holidays, perhaps, but this cold bleak weather is not conducive to thinking of holiday cheer."

"If you hadn't promised Brunhilda that we would scatter her ashes across Germany in her birthday month we would not be here." Perry hid his grin in the scarf he had wrapped high around his neck and chin.

They joined their fellow passengers for the three-hour journey across the channel. Krista received many disapproving stares from the older passengers. The younger crowd, however, thought it was a great lark to see a female dressed in adventurers' gear. They strolled the decks hand in hand, speaking of food they wanted to eat, places they wanted to visit. They gave the impression of what they purported to be – a young couple starting out in life together.

"I want to drive through the Belgium border and on through the German border before we stop for the night." Krista was once more behind the wheel of the campervan. The road leading away from the harbour and towards the border was a good one.

"This is a very strange sensation," Perry said.

"What is?" Krista was concentrating on the road. She was nervous. This would be their first meeting with officialdom.

"We are on the wrong side of the road!" Perry's foot hit the floor, reaching for a non-existent brake.

"It is strange to me too." Krista laughed. "I am driving in what feels like the passenger seat!"

"Keep laughing," Perry said through his teeth. "We are coming up to the border guards."

A guard, a pistol on his hip, stepped into the road and held his hand out in a stop action.

Krista brought the campervan to a smooth halt close to where the glowering guard stood. He stared at the licence plate on the car and a smiling Krista sitting on the wrong side and approached scowling.

"Do you speak French?" He practically barked in

French as soon as Krista had rolled down the driver's window.

"Does not every civilised person?" Krista responded fluently with a wide smile.

"What are you doing here? Where are you going? This is not a good time to travel into Germany." He looked at the couple, shaking his head at their folly. "It could be dangerous." He could say no more but he wished he could order this pair to get back on the road and go home. The border was an uneasy place to work in these troubled times.

"My husband and I are fulfilling a promise I made to my German great-great-grandmother as she lay dying." Krista waved a hand at a smiling Perry.

"You are in a wheelchair." The guard's eyes almost popped out of his head as he leaned in the window to get a better look at the man.

"Oh, he doesn't need that!" Krista gave a delighted thrill of laughter. "The silly man had a riding accident just before our wedding." She pouted delightfully. "I was very cross with him, I can tell you. Can you imagine – taking his horse over the highest fence during the hunt – and right before our wedding!"

"But why the invalid chair?"

"Oh, that is his mother's fussing!" Krista flicked her hair in disgust. "She thought her poor baby would get fatigued walking around on his healing leg."

"*Papers!*" the guard barked. He couldn't stand here listening to this beautiful young girl. He had work to do. He prayed they would travel safely through a country he feared was not safe for anyone these days.

Their papers and campervan were examined before

the guard gave the signal to his fellow guard to lift the barrier. Krista took the papers with a beaming smile for the guard and, with a shouted farewell, turned to drive forward.

"How did I do?" she whispered as they drove slowly along the road separating the guard post on the Belgian side of the border and the German guard post.

"I think you confused that guard. Good for you. Now see if you can do it again."

It was more difficult to confuse the German guard. Krista made much of the fact that her great-grandmother had extracted a promise from her on her deathbed. A promise she was determined to keep. They were eventually allowed through, but the guard was on the telephone to someone as they drove through the barrier and onto German soil.

"I don't know if we got away with that." Perry could not hear what the guard had been saying on the telephone.

"If I did not think it would attract attention I would pull over onto the side of the road and indulge in a fit of the vapours. I have never done such a thing before but there is a first time for everything."

Chapter 5

"We are to drive in the direction of Aachen. There is a forest park slightly off the road where we are to camp. The border between the two countries runs through the forest. We will camp there tonight and drive into Aachen tomorrow." Perry had the map and guidebook on his lap.

"I will be glad to get out and stretch my legs." Krista drove where he directed, longing to get out of the van. She wanted to take a moment to think about the fact that they were in Germany. They had arrived but what awaited them? "We will have to shop for supplies in Aachen tomorrow. We can make a list of our requirements this evening." They were stopped twice on the road by bad-tempered motorcycle guards. The story of Brunhilda was told, the urn displayed and with grunts of disgust they were waved on their way.

When she finally brought the van to a halt by the side of a stream almost hidden by heavy tree branches, Krista was exhausted.

"We need to get set up," Perry almost bounced from the van. "I'll gather firewood. There is no point in using up our supplies when there is an abundance around us. We will have one fire outside this evening and the stove in the van will warm the place enough for us to sleep comfortably."

Krista wanted to roll her eyes to heaven. If this was his idea of comfort, he could keep it. Still, she had agreed to this charade and would not start complaining now. The sum of money she was being paid for her part in this seemed suddenly not quite enough!

Working together, they pulled the awning away from the body of the campervan and set the table and two folding chairs outside. Perry had set up a fireplace of rocks in a circle. He'd picked fallen branches and thick sticks from the floor of the forest. The branches were soon blazing, casting bright light into the darkness. The fire in the van was burning to warm the interior. Krista opened and heated two cans of beef stew. She carried the pot out of the campervan. She put it on a flat rock in the circle around the fire hoping to keep the food hot. She set the table and put a packet of crackers close to hand. It was not fine dining, but they were hungry.

"You could walk through the trees and into Belgium from this spot," Perry, a spoonful of stew held close to his mouth, leaned forward to say. "It might be good to get to know the best route."

Krista too leaned in. "This poor woman we are to meet has been on the run for days. When she reaches us, if she reaches us, I expect her to be completed drained and ready to collapse."

To anyone watching, the couple were having an intimate conversation.

"We may need her to jump out and walk across the border," Perry said. "We could arrange to pick her up on the other side. I would like to have a plan in place for the worst eventuality." He blew on his spoon. "What did you think of the guards who stopped us? Was it my imagination or were they –"

"Prepared to shoot first and ask questions of a corpse?" Krista knew exactly what he meant.

"Something of the sort, yes." Perry smiled. "I would not have stated the matter as you have but they were both more aggressive than I would have thought for guards accustomed to tourists visiting this park."

"We will have a better idea tomorrow when we visit Aachen." Krista wanted to shop for their needs but also get a feel for what was going on in this area. "Listening to gossiping customers should give us information. And the shopkeepers will know what is going on."

"Good God, you don't intend to ask them – do you?"

"Of course not." Krista laughed. "I will be the sweet young English bride complaining about the cruelty of her new husband who expects her to camp out in the forest. Then I will tell anyone who wants to listen all about Brunhilda and her dying wishes."

The following day they were stopped several times by aggressive guards as they drove towards Aachen. Krista enquired about shopping for supplies. She made a point of complaining about the cruel treatment of her new husband and his desire to experience nature in the raw.

In the end they had not dared explore the forest around their camp site for a possible escape route. As they sat by their fire, Perry became convinced that all of the noises they heard were not made by animals. Krista had been happy to stay by the fire. She was not one to step out into the wilderness.

They were given directions to the marketplace by a guard and Krista found a place to park the campervan in one of the laneways leading off the market square.

"You are going to have difficulty walking on these cobblestones," she said, turning off the engine. "You should take your cane, I think. You do not want to stumble."

They locked the van and walked towards the market. They stood for a moment to take in the sheer grandeur of the square. Tall grey granite buildings framed it. The cathedral towered over all, its spread of granite gables like wings greeting all comers. Tall government buildings of breath-taking beauty framed two sides of the square.

They asked directions and visited a nearby bank to change some of their traveller's cheques. The bank clerk was sullen as he practically threw the German marks onto the bank countertop. Krista pretended not to notice his attitude, smiling widely and remarking on the beauty of the building.

They stepped out of the building onto the market square.

"Oh Perry, darling!" Krista gushed loudly in English

as they started to walk between the stalls set out on the square.

There appeared to be a great many armed scowling soldiers examining the market crowd. The atmosphere was heavy, with none of the sounds of laughter and shouted conversations you would expect from such a place.

"Look, Perry, you simply have to try some of these!" She pointed to an array of sausages hanging from the top of a butcher's stall. "Grosmutti loved German sausage. She always told me it was the best in the world. You simply must try it."

She stopped in front of the stall, beaming a wide smile.

There were no words of greeting from the butcher.

"Everything looks wonderful," she said to him in fluent German.

"It is made with pig!" he barked.

"So?" Krista shrugged. "Should that be a problem?" She knew Jewish people did not eat pork.

She was aware of a couple of soldiers stepping close to the stall.

"How do you sell the sausage? We are travelling and cannot store a great deal but I must introduce my husband to the foods my German relatives love so much."

"You can buy it sliced."

"Wonderful!"

There was no curiosity about the two foreigners standing in front of his stall. He did not question or remark upon her knowledge of his language. He just sliced the sausage, wrapped it and handed it over.

That attitude and the close attention of the soldiers continued as Krista flitted around the market, pulling

Perry along behind her. She visited the baker's stall and clapped her hands in delight to see the selection of breads and cakes.

She spent time in front of a stall selling baskets. She couldn't make up her mind and ran her fingers over the items on offer. She questioned the stallholder about her goods. She purchased one of the shopping baskets.

She insisted on buying a coffee percolator and ground coffee, proclaiming to all at the stall that her husband had only tea on board his campervan. She drifted from stall to stall, complaining bitterly in German about her husband and his expectations of his new bride.

Krista was acting for all she was worth. Her stomach was tied in knots. The atmosphere in the market was frightening. She wanted to hunch her shoulders and hurry away. The shoppers walked along with their heads bowed. There was no exchange of gossip as people stopped to buy their household needs.

The soldiers, travelling in pairs, glared and marched around the square as if they ruled the world. Perhaps they did. No one seemed willing to attract their attention.

Perry accompanied Krista with a besotted smile on his face – ready to hand over the money for whatever his darling wanted. He appeared to be unaware or unable to understand the insults directed at him by the muttering soldiers.

"Do you want to visit the cathedral, darling?" Perry asked in English. He didn't think there was anything more Krista could buy. "I would like to sit down for a moment."

"Oh, my poor darling!" Krista was instantly all remorse. She reached up to press a kiss on his cheek. "What am I thinking of? Dragging you around after

me! You are so brave. You should have said something."
She fluttered frantically.

They walked slowly towards the entrance of the
magnificent edifice. Perry offered to carry her basket of
shopping but she refused to relinquish it. They were
aware of the stares being directed at them but
continued to portray a young English couple totally
besotted with each other and unaware of the world
around them.

The interior of the cathedral welcomed them. Krista
wanted to collapse onto the nearest bench. She could not.
There were people in the cathedral praying. She helped
Perry onto one of the benches. She put her basket of
shopping beside him then stood for a while, staring
around her at the wealth and beauty of the place.

She joined Perry on the bench and they sat for a
while, holding hands and looking around.

"We should get back on the road," Perry whispered.

They stood to leave, Krista stepping out first, her
shopping in hand. Perry followed her. An old man
passing with his head bowed, hands clenched in prayer,
bumped into Perry rather violently. He grabbed Perry's
shoulders to steady him, apologising loudly in German.
He used his work-roughened hands to keep Perry
steady on his feet and muttered in English, "*Get her out
of here. Get away. Go home while you still can.*"

He apologised again in German and walked from
the cathedral, muttering about stupid Englishmen
under his breath. The words could be clearly heard as
the acoustics in the cathedral were excellent. The old
man knew what he was doing obviously, as his whisper
to Perry hadn't even been heard by Krista.

"Are you alright?" Krista asked.

"I am fine, but I really would like to get on the road." Perry gripped the handle of his cane and walked, with Krista making noises of concern at his side, out of the building and over the cobbles to where they had left the campervan.

There were four soldiers standing around the van.

"Gentlemen, hello – may we help you?" Krista called in German, the wide smile on her face almost hurting.

They turned at her words and her heart sank even further at their cold expressions.

With hardly a word, they then subjected the van and the travellers to an examination that had Krista biting her tongue. There was no need to pull everything from the storage areas and throw them around. When one held the urn in the air in a threatening way, she burst into tears and loud hysterical sobbing – which wasn't difficult to do in the circumstances.

"*She was so proud to be German!*" Krista stood with tears flowing down her cheeks. She had been telling the story of Brunhilda to the soldiers as they tore apart their little campervan. "She insisted I and all of her family learn to speak her mother tongue." She swiped frantically at her cheeks, ignoring the handkerchief Perry tried to pass to her. "She was so proud of the fact that I resemble her. She wanted to spend eternity flying over her beloved country!"

One of the soldiers stopped tearing at the contents of her Louis Vuitton luggage and asked, "Where did you say she was born?"

"*I didn't!*" Krista wailed, wanting to tell the man to

get his hands off her undergarments. "You never asked!"

"*You said she was born around here!*" another soldier shouted out.

"*I did not!*" Krista wailed. "*Are you not listening to me?*"

Perry had to turn his head away. Krista was playing her part to perfection. He wanted to applaud. The situation was frightening. The place they parked was an artery leading to the market square yet not one person walked along its length while the soldiers held them there.

"*I said she loved this area!*" Krista was giving it all she had. She clenched her fists and shouted at the ignorant louts. "*She told me the men of the region were all that was charming and gallant! It would break her heart to see you behaving so rudely!*" The words might be all that was silly, but she was at least able to shriek out her fury.

"Dear Lord, Perry!" Krista gasped when they had repacked the campervan and taken to the road. "Things are much worse than we were led to believe. The people here are terrified."

"That was some performance back there." Perry too was shocked by their morning's experience. "I didn't know whether to laugh or applaud." He leaned in to touch her shoulder with his. "I will tell you though. I would never marry a woman like you. I could never trust you!"

They laughed until they cried, releasing the tension they had been under.

They drove along, searching for a camping site for

the night. Neither mentioned their orders of remaining in the same camping site for two nights. They neither of them wanted to return to the forest.

"It was brave of that old man to warn me away." Perry had told her what he had said.

"His English was good. Maybe he was a soldier in the Great War."

They talked for a while about this and that, each concerned for the other and their safety.

"Perry, how is Gisele to make her way to us if she is subjected to the kind of treatment we have received?" She looked over at him before returning her attention to the road. "We have each other for company and support but she is alone and scared."

"What will be, will be." Perry had no other answer.

"Yes, indeed … but I pity the poor woman."

After a while Perry said, "Krista, do these roads seem superior to you?"

"What do you mean?"

"Well, you are the one driving but they seem to me to be in excellent shape. In fact, they look almost new." Then it dawned on him. "Dear God – of course – they're for troop movement!"

Chapter 6

Perry left the van, taking care not to wake Krista yet – the poor girl was exhausted. He walked into the forest and moved carefully along, enjoying the sounds of nature around him as the day dawned. He stopped occasionally to pick up sticks and thick fallen branches for the fire. This was the third campsite he had set up. They would break it down today and move on. What they had seen and heard needed to be reported to the powers that be. The aggression in the air was oppressive.

He used one of the branches as a walking stick and continued to explore the forest. He soon became uneasy. He felt as if there were eyes upon him. He had felt this way ever since they reached Germany.

He carried the wood back to their campsite and

started a fire in the pit he had dug. He would let the fire die down before brewing a pot of coffee, slicing some of the bread they had bought in Dormagen yesterday and toasting it. With a little butter and jam they would have a meal.

He sat in one of the chairs they had left under the awning, watching the fire burn down. He hated to wake Krista but they needed to pack up and get back on the road.

"Perry, is it morning already?" Krista bolted upright at the sound of the door opening. The cold bit as soon as the sleeping bag fell away from her.

"It is indeed, sleepyhead," Perry kept his eyes away from her. He stepped carefully around her. She was taking up most of the floor space. He stepped quickly to the little kitchen, removing items he needed. "I have the fire going outside. I am going to make a pot of coffee and toast while you wake up. Join me when you are ready."

It took three trips but he soon had everything he needed to hand.

As soon as Perry closed the campervan door behind him, Krista fought her way out of her sleeping bag. She ached in every bone in her body. She had never felt so cold and tired in her life. She pulled on her outer garments – which she was coming to hate – and used the campervan toilet. When she was ready, she stepped out into the freezing cold morning.

"We can't go on like this," Perry said as soon as they were both clutching mugs of coffee. The heat from the mugs was very welcome.

Krista leaned in to her mug, enjoying the aroma of coffee and the warming steam. She was afraid to open her mouth. She did not want to be the one to admit defeat.

"There is simply no way anyone could find us out in the middle of nowhere as we appear to be." Perry was frustrated. They had been driving back and forth within a wide circle for days. The cold was deepening and if he wasn't mistaken snow was on the way.

"Captain Waters appeared to believe she could find us. We are her best hope. I hate to leave anyone to the mercy of the soldiers and guards we have been encountering."

It seemed that every road they drove down they encountered more and more soldiers. They, all of them, seemed to take a perverse delight in stopping the campervan and demanding papers and explanations. The very daring demanded they search the campervan. They took no care of the items packed so carefully within the small space. Perry and Krista were forced to spend time returning everything to its place when the bully boys gave up on their idea of fun. They stood around the van and laughed to see the pair restoring order to the chaos they had created.

"Today we will drive to Dusseldorf and take a room in a hotel," Perry stated.

"Perry …" Krista didn't know what to say. It would be such a relief to be out of the cold. *She could have a bath*. She almost clapped her hands but didn't want to let go of the warm mug.

"We have given it our best shot, Krista," Perry too longed for a bath and the chance to sleep in a warm soft bed. "We have driven past so many train stations and bus stations I am almost blind from searching faces without appearing to!"

It was his job to search for the woman and take mental note of all around them while Krista kept her eyes on the road. Waters could not allow them to take the photograph of his sister – it would be too risky. Perry and Krista had done their best to memorise Gisele's face.

"We need a break from all this, Krista, to boost our morale."

"But …" she tried to object but her heart wasn't in it.

"Krista," Perry swivelled in his deckchair to reach for the coffee pot sitting in the hot ashes to one side of the fire, "you have a career in front of you as a writer of fiction." He laughed while refilling their mugs. He returned the pot to the ashes before throwing the last of the wood on the fire. "You have told so many stories of Brunhilda Alvensleben and her many beau that I feel I know the woman. I could almost feel the waves from the pleasure cruiser under my feet when you regaled that last lot of guards."

"I was afraid, Perry." Krista sipped the coffee. He had offered to make toast but she couldn't eat a thing right now. "It breaks my heart to see the beauty all around us. Cologne was a wonderland for the eyes, yet you could sense that everyone was afraid. We need to leave Germany and return home. I sometimes feel as if I have a ticking clock inside my head warning me to run." It was time and past to admit how terrified, tired and miserable she was. The effort of constantly putting a smile on her face and greeting those soldiers and guards as if she did not fear them was taking its toll.

"I too have had enough," Perry threw the dregs of his coffee on the fire. They hadn't eaten the bread he had carried out for toast. It didn't matter. Nothing mattered at the moment as much as packing up and getting on the road.

They were old hands at the chores that needed to be completed before they moved on from their campsites. They could be packed up in little time.

They didn't need words between them as Krista returned and stored all items in the campervan. Perry threw earth on the fire and carefully checked to insure there were no sparks remaining. He would allow the stones that surrounded the fire to cool while he rolled the awning back into the side of the van. By the time they left it would be almost as if they were never here.

"You have not enjoyed camping at all, have you, Krista?" Perry asked as they motored along the smooth road.

"If Brunhilda had been born in June," she took her eyes off the road for a moment to share a laugh with him, "I am sure the journey would have been delightful. We have camped in areas which are so beautiful. In the sunshine I am sure I would delight in skipping gaily along but in the cold … *mon Dieu*, it is miserable!"

"We have not been able to escape each other either." Perry was keeping a close eye on the area they passed through. There were a lot of people on the road travelling to work. Factories billowed out black smoke into the air. It did not appear Germany was suffering the same lack of industry as the rest of the world. The economic depression had cut deep into the life of English working men and women. But it would appear everyone in Germany – or at least the area they had passed through – had more work than they had hours.

"I am proud of both of us." Krista too was noticing the trucks carrying payloads of coal along the route. "We have made a true effort to remain polite and sane." She once again took her eyes from the road. "It has been difficult at times."

"Keep your eyes on the road and head with all speed to Dusseldorf, madam. I want a bath and a soft bed."

They laughed together. They were becoming expert at presenting an image of carefree youth to anyone who might care to watch and wonder.

"You will have more of an audience there as you heap coals of abuse upon my poor innocent head for bringing you on such a dreadful honeymoon."

"I will give some thought to the abuse I mean to mete out!" She had been bemoaning her lot for so long she was tired of the sound of her own voice.

"Krista," Perry didn't move in his seat but his voice was sharp, "there are a lot of trucks heading off the main road in that direction." He used his hand, hidden under the campervan's body to point to a line of trucks waiting to exit the road they were on to link up with another. "We need to follow that road and see what is going on."

"Some of those trucks are filled with soldiers." Krista too had been taking note. "It would be dangerous to follow along while there are so many waiting to exit. We need to find somewhere to wait and make the connection to the other road when this lot have cleared."

"Slow down." Perry sat forward. "Turn in there." He pointed.

Krista didn't question him. She was used to him giving directions. She drove off the main road into what appeared to be a way station – there was a restaurant and garage with several petrol pumps. There was even a row of public toilets. She pulled the campervan up to one of the petrol pumps and turned off the engine with a sigh of relief. She intended to use the public toilets no matter how dire they might be. She stepped out of the van on one side and Perry on the other.

"*Darling!*"

Perry's voice stopped her in her tracks.

She'd been preparing to push through the interested crowd and sprint to the toilets. She wanted to inspect the interior. If there was hot running water she intended to freshen up.

In English he said loudly, "Will you tell this man what we need before you disappear, please."

"Sorry, darling," Krista said in English. "I was so eager to check out what appears to be a plumbed-in toilet I forgot my manners. What do we need?"

"Ask this chap if there is someone who can wash the van down and wax it." He patted the side of the van fondly. "We have put the old girl through her paces."

"Perhaps I could assist?" A man they had not noticed stepped into view.

He was an attractive older man with grey shading the blonde hair over his ears. His blue eyes had lines around them like those of a man used to the outdoors. He was dressed expensively and gave the impression of being comfortable with his place in the world. "I can translate your needs," he gestured towards the attendant with one elegant hand, "while your wife tends to her own needs."

"*Herr Count!*" The attendant clicked his heels

together and gave the '*Heil Hitler*' salute.

"You run along, darling," Perry said. "This gentleman will translate for me."

"I shan't be long!" Krista took to her heels. She noticed the presence of the man the attendant had called Herr Count seemed to be affecting the behaviour of the men around her. There were no nasty comments and offensive suggestions offered as she sought a free public toilet.

"Johann Graf Benz, Count Westheimer." The man introduced himself with a smile. He clicked his heels. "At your service."

"Peregrine Fotheringham-Carter." Perry took the hand the German held out and shook. "Perry."

"Delighted to meet you," Johann said in excellent English. "How may I help?"

"I thought to have the van washed and waxed while my wife and I have something to eat. My poor darling, I am afraid, is ready to commit murder. It hasn't been the most comfortable of trips." Perry laughed lightly.

"It is a very unusual vehicle." Johann appeared to have all the time in the world to stand and talk. "It attracted my attention."

"I commissioned her." Perry gave the van another pat. "She has been a little wonder on this her maiden voyage."

"Would you show me around?" Johann Graf Benz gestured to the van.

"Should I move it out of the way first?" Perry looked around the busy way station. "We are blocking the petrol pump."

"No need." The Count barked orders to the attendant

before gesturing to the door of the van. The attendant rushed away to serve another driver.

"If you would care to step into the van," Perry held the door open. "It is tight quarters. I will stand out here and answer any questions you might have."

"Why, it is all ship-shape!" Johann exclaimed as he accepted the invitation to examine the van interior. He opened a door. "A toilet." With his hand on a built-in cupboard he turned to look at Perry. "May I?"

"Be our guest."

"It is almost like being on a small boat!" Johann delighted in poking his nose into every feature.

"I thought the same thing myself." Perry stood smiling on the forecourt while yet another German examined his vehicle. This man, however, was a far different sort than the bully boys they had encountered so far. He was far more dangerous.

In the meantime, Krista had been fortunate in that a cleaning woman was leaving one of the many toilets in the cement-block building. The woman gestured to the toilet she had just cleaned, suggesting Krista could make use of it before the men had a chance to turn it back into a pigsty. The toilet was a luxury to Krista after days of using the van. And miracle of miracles, it had running hot water!

Krista ran across the cement surface back towards the campervan. She passed Perry with a wave and jumped into the van's interior.

"Herr Count," she had heard how the attendant addressed this man, "I do not mean to be rude, but I have a lovely woman holding closed the door to a freshly cleaned bathroom. I am going to take full advantage!"

She bent to pull her vanity case out of the fitted wardrobe and ran back outside. "Perry, it has hot running water!" She shouted over her shoulder as she ran.

"You are a fortunate man." The Count stepped down beside Perry. "I have had ladies express less pleasure at the gift of diamonds." He clapped Perry on the shoulder, laughing loudly.

Chapter 7

The two men were sitting in the busy café/restaurant drinking coffee and smoking the Count's cigars, at a table hastily offered up to the Count by saluting men. Thanks to his translation assistance, the campervan was taken away to be washed and waxed, the water supply topped up and the spirit cannister for the cooking stove changed.

"So, Fotheringham-Carter," Johann Graf Benz said. "Your family are, I think, sailors." Johann smiled at Perry's surprise. "I have competed against men of that name in regattas."

"My father and brothers." Perry laughed. "Their passion is sailing and the sea."

"But not your own?"

"I sail but my first love is horses." Perry tried not to clench his teeth around the cigar. The man sitting across from him was a naval officer or he'd eat his hat. He recognised the look in his eyes and the set of his shoulders.

"I too ..."

"Pardon me." Perry began to stand. He had seen Krista standing on the forecourt, looking around for the campervan.

"No need." Johann clicked his fingers and barked a command to a waiter who hurried to open the door of the restaurant. The waiter ran over to Krista and pointed to where the two men were visible through the tall windows of the restaurant.

"Perry, darling!" Krista, vanity case in hand, hurried to the table.

The two men stood at her approach.

"When I couldn't see the campervan I thought you had deserted me." She giggled. "I wouldn't blame you for running from a nagging wife." She smiled at the man with Perry. "Hello again, Herr Count."

"Frau Fotheringham-Carter." Johann clicked his heels and took her free hand, carrying it to his lips.

"Call me Krista, please! Otherwise I shall be looking over my shoulder for my mother-in-law!" She smiled widely, all bright blue eyes and innocent charm.

"Sit here, darling." Perry took the vanity case and put it on the floor. He pulled out a chair. The two men waited until Krista was seated before sitting.

"Have you ordered something to eat, darling?" Krista shook out her napkin.

"I thought I'd wait for you to see what it was you would like," Perry said.

"They have wonderful fish –" Johann stopped speaking when Krista began to laugh, immediately joined by Perry.

"I am so sorry, Herr Count!" Krista waved her napkin in the air, tears of amusement in her eyes.

"Johann, please." He exuded charm.

"Johann, thank you." Krista gave a jerk of her head in his direction. "You could not know but we," she waved a hand between herself and Perry, "have been having heated discussions about Perry's wish to fish. I could not bear it. I like fish. In fact, it is one of my favourites – but lightly broiled on a plate!" She buried her face in her napkin, shoulders shaking with suppressed amusement.

"So, no hunting." Johann shared an amused look with Perry over Krista's bowed head.

"No gun," Perry said.

"I thought you were living off the land when I saw your sweet little campervan." Johann raised an eyebrow.

"No, no!" Krista objected. "We have been living off canned stew."

"You are a fortunate man, Perry," Johann said. "To have a woman willing to accompany you camping."

"No, Johann." Krista wiped her eyes with the napkin and stared earnestly into Johann's pale blue eyes. "I am the one who is fortunate. Perry has planned all of this," she waved in the direction of the forecourt vaguely, "for me …"

Then the story of Brunhilda was told once more.

Perry put his hand on Krista's arm and stopped her in her storytelling from time to time. He asked Johann's advice about the food on offer. They ordered and were served while Krista continued to entertain the Count and anyone listening with tales of her great-great-grandmother. Perry added a word where he could. He had heard the tale of Brunhilda so often he could join in Krista's story.

"Brunhilda Alvensleben," Johann said when Krista paused in her story to sample the food. "I wonder if my grandfather would have known her?"

"It would have to be your great-grandfather, I believe," Perry said. "Brunhilda was one hundred and three years old when she died two years ago."

"That is a great age." Johann shook his head.

Krista was enjoying the hot dish she had been served. It was hot, nourishing and delicious, with dumplings that were light and fluffy.

"She outlived everyone of her age group." Krista blotted her lips with her napkin. "It was very sad."

The three settled in to enjoy their meal, exchanging polite chit-chat from time to time. The meal was consumed, coffee served and with Krista's permission cigars were lit. The garage attendant entered the restaurant and presented Perry with a bill for the work done on the campervan.

"It has been a pleasure meeting you both," Johann said as the attendant left. "But I must continue on my journey."

"Before you leave us, Johann," Krista said, "my darling husband is booking a hotel for us this evening. We had hoped to reach Dusseldorf and book a room. Can you recommend somewhere?"

"Yes, of course ... but let me settle the bill ..."

Johann reached for his wallet, but Perry stopped him, insisting he should pay for the meal.

Johann agreed with a smile. "There is a road off this one." He pointed in the direction of the road that interested Perry and Krista. "If you follow it you will come to the harbour. There is a grand hotel overlooking the water that I believe will please you."

"Bliss!" Krista clapped her hands. "I cannot wait to have a bath."

"I shall not say I shall think of you in your bath." Johann stood and clicked his heels. "It would not be the act of a gentleman."

He left them, laughing.

"That was frightening," Perry said when they were once more on the road.

"Yes, indeed," Krista agreed. "The Count was all that is charming, but I got the impression we were being skilfully interrogated."

"He knew my father and brothers," Perry said.

"The ties between Germany and Britain are strong." Krista had to pay close attention to the road. The number of trucks sharing the road was impressive. "If it comes to war there will be a lot of heartbreak."

"It is no longer a question of 'if', Krista. It is when. What we have seen in our travels has been – to me anyway – clear indication that Germany is gearing up for war. There are too many soldiers on the road. Too many factories producing items that when assembled could well be machines of war. We cannot close our eyes to all."

"I agree. Look – what are those strange-looking ships?"

They were approaching the harbour, Perry keeping a lookout for the hotel the Count had recommended.

"Sweet Lord!" Perry pressed at the dash. "Drive very slowly." He removed a pair of the smallest binoculars that Krista had ever seen from a hidden compartment. He put them to his eyes and his gasp of horror was clearly heard. "They are submarines, Krista. The man-made sharks of the sea. There are far too many of them." He lowered the glasses. "Our navy will be sitting ducks with those hunting them." He felt sick to his stomach to think of men being forced to face the sea with hunters beneath them.

"Smile!" Krista gave a sickly smile herself.

They were attracting attention from the men travelling to work on the docks. A guard stepped into the path of the van, his arm up in the halt position.

Krista put her head out of the driver's window and shamelessly used the Count's name. She gave the address of the hotel the Count had recommended and was given directions without a great deal of bother.

"It is just as I thought," Perry said as Krista prepared to turn the van around. "Did you notice the guard's reaction to the Count's name? He is an officer in the German navy. I am sure of it now."

"Why did he send us down this road, I wonder?" said Krista. "He must have realised that we would see all these submarines. Strange."

Perry shot her a look. "Do you think he did it deliberately? That he wanted us to see them?"

"For what reason?"

"I don't know." Perry shook his head, puzzled.

He wanted to telephone his father but knew he

could not. It would endanger the Count and themselves. He would have to wait until he returned home to share this information. What seaman would not be sickened at the carnage those submarines could cause – and so close to the channel that separated the Continent from Britain? The navy must be warned.

Krista stood in the luxurious foyer of the hotel. They made a sorry sight in their camping clothes. A porter stood behind her with a trolley holding their luggage. She was not needed for translation here – the male receptionist spoke fluent English. Perry asked for laundry services straight away. He booked a suite for them with attached bathroom and a fireplace in the living room of the suite. Krista almost swooned at the thought of such luxury. He gave the Count's name with a smile when asked how he had heard of the hotel. It was all very convivial.

"Can you recommend somewhere my wife can have her hair styled?" Perry asked as he signed a great number of traveller's cheques.

"The hotel has a spa, sir." The receptionist watched closely as Perry continued to turn pages in his folder of cheques. "This area is known for its healing waters and spa treatments." He looked down his nose at Perry as if he should have known this about an area he was visiting. "I can make a booking for your wife if that is your wish?"

"Yes, please." Krista stepped forward to twine her arm through Perry's. "I would love some pampering, darling."

"It is the least you deserve after days of camping, my love."

"The spa is enjoyed by gentlemen also." The receptionist looked at Perry's bristled chin, untidy hair and rough clothing.

"Capital," Perry smiled. "Please make bookings for both of us."

They discussed timing, with Krista insisting she needed a long bath before she could think of anything else. She fussed aloud about getting their soiled clothing to the laundry woman as soon as possible. It would take time to dry the items. If there was someone listening, he would be very bored with their inane chatter.

Perry stood in the wide window, his arm around Krista's shoulder, as they admired the view of the harbour.

"I need a bath." Krista turned away from the view of a line of very menacing-looking machines that were docked nose to nose along both sides of the harbour walls.

Perry followed her to the bathroom and closed the door behind him. He put a finger to his lips when Krista began to object. He put the plug in the bath and turned both taps on full.

When the water was flowing freely, he said, "I may be seeing shadows where there are none, but it would be very easy to put a receiver somewhere in these rooms. It would be a simple matter to have someone listen to everything we say. The noise of the water will block our words. I believe."

"God, Perry!" Krista sat on the side of the bath, her head in her hands.

"We cannot continue to drive around this area in the

hopes that we will make contact." He did not mention the woman they sought. Better to err on the side of caution. "We have information we must get back to those in command of our forces."

"Let me have my bath." Krista stood to add some of the scented sachets that were offered to the hotel guests to her bath water. She reduced the flow of the cold water. The last thing she wanted was a tepid bath. "We can do nothing at this moment."

"We need to sort our laundry." Perry opened the bathroom door as he spoke.

He took the tiny but powerful binoculars from his trouser pocket and keeping his body hidden behind the long curtains that framed the window he made a close examination of the docks.

"Did the receptionist say the people from the laundry would come by or do we need to telephone down when I have the laundry ready?" Krista was speaking to Perry's back as she pulled items from their haversacks. She kept her voice light and unworried. "I love your mother dearly, darling, but the clothes she chose for me – they are far from my preferred style of dress. Do you think the laundry will be able to launder this waterproof material?" She ran into the bathroom to shut off the taps.

In the basement spa of the hotel Krista was primped and oiled. She was determined to enjoy the experience. She had seen the prices and knew she might never be able to afford such a thing again.

Perry was in the gentlemen's section being groomed.

Krista was led from small treatment room to small

treatment room by a smiling attendant. She had to wait sometimes, wrapped in the hotel's dressing gown with other women. They were offered the water the spa town was known for while they waited. She kept her eyes closed and her mouth shut. She listened to the buzz of conversation around her with knots in her stomach. The women were all exchanging hateful stories about Jewish people. She had to hide her clenched fists in the deep pockets of her dressing gown. It took almost everything she had not to gasp at the vitriol being poured on the heads of innocent people.

One would talk about the luxury apartment her Jewish neighbours lived in while some relative was living in a garret. It was the fault of the Jews of course.

Krista listened and wanted to shout her horror to the sky. They were speaking with such venom about Jews being forced out of their businesses by loyal Germans. The Jews too were German. Could these women not see that?

She was glad when the stylist put curlers in her hair and put her under a dryer. She could no longer hear the conversations around her. She closed her eyes, allowing the warm air to caress her face while she tried to understand how a nation of educated people could be so misled.

"Look at you!" Perry picked Krista up and swung her around the room to delighted squeals from her. "My God, Krista," he whispered into her ear while she continued to make sounds of delight, "the world is running mad. The things I have heard." Then aloud he said, "There is the woman I married. You look wonderful."

"Good enough to be taken to dinner?" She shook her head and tried to communicate her own horror without words. Perhaps no one was listening to them, but it did not do to take chances.

"I want to show you off to the world!" Perry cried dramatically.

Chapter 8

"Darling, I have been making enquiries." Perry tucked into the selection of breads and cheese that comprised breakfast. The dining room set aside for guests to break their fast was smaller than the room they had dined in the previous evening. The heat from the fire was very welcome. The view through a nearby window was of a dismal grey day.

"Try this one." Krista held out the cheese platter, pointing with the cheese knife. "It is delicious."

They had returned to the hotel after an early morning stroll around the harbour. She was glad to be in out of the biting wind.

"Darling, pay attention!" Perry was very conscious of the waiter standing by the coffee urn, a white linen cloth over his arm. "The last place Brunhilda asked you to visit." He bit into crunchy bread. "Herr Count assured me that the area you seek is marshland. A great deal of it is under water!"

"I am so sorry I asked you to help me keep my promise to Grandmother Brunhilda." Krista wanted to get in the van and drive straight to the border. "It is her birthday today, November 10th, you know."

"I had forgotten." Perry admired the figure Krista presented, sitting across the table from him. She had insisted on wearing one of the charming outfits she had packed for this journey. Under her slacks, he knew she was wearing her last fresh pair of long winter undergarments. She refused to wear the dainties that had been much handled by German guards. The men had taken a perverse pleasure from handling the delicate items.

"She would have been one hundred and five today." Krista was playing for the waiter who, she felt, was paying a great deal of attention to what was being said at their table. She allowed the sadness she felt at failing to rescue poor Gisele Waters to show – tears tracked down cheeks glowing from the beauty treatments she'd received at the spa.

"My poor darling!" Perry, dressed in his Savile Row suit, took a white handkerchief from his inside jacket pocket. He stood and gently dried her tears. "I do not mean to upset you. Please, don't cry."

The urn containing the ashes was almost empty. They had made a production of spreading the ashes into the wind wherever they had stopped. He would be glad to see the last of them. He pressed a kiss into her forehead before taking his seat.

* * *

"Drive to Essen." Perry was once more in his wheeled passenger-seat, the map spread out before him. "It is a short journey from here." It would take them less than an hour to reach Essen. It was one of the areas mentioned in particular by Captain Waters. They were determined to do all they could to allow Gisele Waters to reach them but the trip they had planned would lead them directly to the German-Belgium border. It was time to leave.

Krista was once more wearing her oiled clothing. The laundry had been returned and packed. She was happy to be heading in the direction of the border. The tension and fear of the people they had passed today was making her physically ill. As a child she had learned to judge the atmosphere in the Dumas household. It gave her time to get out of the way of flying fists and shouting voices. She could almost taste the fear in the atmosphere in Dusseldorf.

"Would you think that I was losing my senses if I told you I want to find a deep dark hole and hide?"

"Not in the least," Perry said. "There are far too many soldiers on the road." A troop-carrying truck passed their van with an angry blare of its horn. "The people are afraid. You can sense it everywhere we have visited. I will be glad to get you out of here and back to Britain. This is no place for a woman." He was thinking of Gisele Waters, hating the thought of leaving her to the mercy of the soldiers.

They motored along, saying little but each paying attention to the vehicles that passed them. They reached Essen and here too they could feel the tension. They had agreed to stock up with foodstuffs at the market.

Krista parked in a side street and, with her basket in hand, they entered the marketplace. They both had to work hard not to react to what they were seeing around them. As they purchased bread, sandwich fillings and cans to restock their larder, the pushing and verbal abuse towards some of the customers was shocking.

"We should stop here for lunch." Perry wanted to pick Krista up and run. He doubted he could eat but they needed to get out of the market crowd. He pointed to a nearby restaurant.

"A cup of coffee and a warm place to sit out of this wind would be welcome," Krista agreed.

They both forced food down while watching the view outside the tall windows of the restaurant. There was actual violence taking place towards customers. The soldiers marching around were turning a blind eye – some even laughed. The time it took to eat the food and pay seemed an eternity. They left the restaurant arm in arm and, keeping well out of the way of the pushing crowd, walked towards where they had parked.

"*Perry!*" Krista began to run.

The campervan was tilting to one side. Reaching it, she rounded it to stare in disbelief at its tyres.

She darted back around it to shout "*Perry! Someone has slashed two of our tyres!*"

He was making his way with slow careful steps over the uneven cobbles. He halted in shock.

A man saw their plight and walked over to them. He

was so wrapped up against the cold, it was impossible to make out his features.

He shook his head for a moment before saying in English, "My brother has a garage and workshop on the outskirts of town. He may have tyres that will fit."

"How can we get there?" Perry felt an itch at the back of his neck. Someone had written in white paint *English Go Home* along the side of the van. He touched it gingerly – it was whitewash and should be easy to remove. A small blessing. They needed to leave this place. "We have one spare tyre but who carries two!"

"I will telephone my brother. He has a recovery vehicle." He stood with his hands on his hips, glaring at them. "But it will cost you."

"Thank you. That would be a great help." Perry began to take the spare wheel and tools to change it from the van. Whoever had slit the tyres had done it on one side of the van, probably to keep out of sight. The recovery van would lift the van onto its back wheels and pull it along the road. They needed a good wheel on each side for that.

The man hurried away to find a telephone. Krista and Perry put the articles they purchased away before both turning their attention to changing the tyre. There were a great many ribald remarks from passing soldiers, but no one offered to help or bothered them further. They soon had the wheel changed, tools returned to their place and the van ready to move. All they could do was sit inside the cold van and keep watch against further vandalism. They were both praying that the stranger was really going to telephone someone to help them.

At the sound of a large vehicle approaching they jumped to their feet. When they opened the van door and stepped outside, they discovered the man had been as good as his word. He grunted instructions to them in English.

The van was soon standing on its two back wheels, attached to the recovery vehicle. The stranger jumped into the truck beside his brother. Krista and Perry were told to jump into the back of the recovery vehicle, dangerously close to the crane with its heavy chains that would pull the van along behind them. The sight of the two English people sitting in the cold with their van being towed along caused a great deal of amusement among soldiers and passing strangers.

It took some time to drive through Essen towards the outskirts of the city. The garage was in a remote area set well back from the road with tall trees surrounding it. When the recovery vehicle stopped, Perry and Krista were both frozen.

"I cannot offer you a hand out," the helpful stranger muttered into the scarf surrounding his neck.

Krista was taken aback.

"There is a fire in the shack." He gave a jerk of his chin in the direction of the large barnlike building to one side at the back of the lot. "Get inside before you freeze." He turned his attention to helping his brother.

Krista and Perry climbed out of the truck and walked towards the barn. The front was open with cars and trucks parked inside. There was a three-sided shack off to one side inside the larger building. They walked towards it, almost groaning when the heat from a closed freestanding fire reached them.

"I am sorry about your tyres," the man said, entering the shack. "It was the only way I could think of to get you to where I needed you." He removed his muffler and hat, revealing the man they had met in the cathedral in Aachen. The one who warned Perry to get Krista out of Germany. "You speak German, yes?" he asked in English, looking at Krista.

"Yes. I am –"

"*No names!*" The man barked. "You may call me Jan." He jerked his head towards the driver of the recovery vehicle when he entered the shack. "He is not really my brother but it will be understood that I expect to make money out of the idiot Englishers who are wandering around an area that *is dangerous to all!*" He shouted so loudly that veins stood up on his forehead. "You will ignore what he says."

The other man began to make telephone calls in search of replacement tyres. His words in German were insulting to both of them. He expressed glee at the amount of money he was going to take from the stupid foreigners.

"I am afraid this is going to take more time than I would like." Jan shook his head sadly. "Slitting your tyres was a spur-of-the-moment action. I needed to get you both out of the market and somewhere safe. It is dangerous to be on Germany's roads at the moment. I told you once before, *you must leave here.*"

"That was our intention until you slit our tyres!" Perry snapped.

"You cannot travel the roads this evening!" Jan huffed. "There are things happening. I cannot believe you are not aware." He hung his head for a moment. "I am ashamed of my countrymen right now. They are shooting and setting fire to shops, homes, displacing men, women and children. It is madness."

"Why would you help us?" Krista asked.

"Because of me." A voice came out of the darkness.

A woman clad all in black, an old-fashioned hat pulled low on her head, was slowly revealed. "I needed to contact you."

"You need to rest!" Jan hurried over to the swaying figure. He took her gently by the arm and led her to the only chair in the shack.

"My God!" Perry gasped when the woman's features were revealed in the light from the fire. The face was a feminine copy of her twin brother's. "Gisele Waters."

Gisele ignored their surprise. She was so grateful for the help her dear friend was giving her but their presence here endangered him.

"Do you have any food in that travelling wagon of yours?" Jan hadn't dared bring food to the garage in case it was noted.

"Yes, of course." Krista had been momentarily frozen in shock. "I will brew a pot of coffee and heat up a few cans of stew. We have plenty of bread."

"*No!*" Jan barked. "Carry all you need in a basket into the garage. You must not be seen to be serving food and drink to anyone here. We are to be enemies."

Krista ran from the garage, making a mental list of all she would need. They had plenty of food. They had just restocked.

"How on earth did you get here?" Perry asked the woman sagging in the chair.

"I walked through nightmares." Gisele closed her eyes against the sights she had seen. "I took night trains. It is not safe to be on the streets after dark. What I have seen …" Tears flowed freely down her chalky cheeks. "They set fire to buildings. They pulled men, women and children into the street and laughed."

"Who did?" Perry demanded when the words stopped.

"Soldiers, brave German soldiers and people – neighbours shouted abuse and laughed. It was unbearable and all I could do was crouch in fear and watch." She buried her face in her hands and sobbed.

"When did this happen?" Perry asked.

"Last night. I know not where I was. I have been walking for what feels like days, hiding and scurrying like an animal." She let her head fall to the back of the chair. "I thought to walk across the border through one of the many out-of-the-way places but everywhere I went I found soldiers stringing barbed wire." She looked at Perry. "I could not believe it when my friend Jan told me he had seen you both days ago in Aachen. I lost all hope. It was sheer chance that Jan heard of your presence in the market square. Why on earth did you return to this area?"

"Your brother made a point of mentioning Essen many times." Perry was aware of Krista running back and forth between the garage and the campervan. The welcome smell of coffee was beginning to drift towards the shack. "We are heading towards the border but we thought to check this area out one more time."

"Thank God you did," Gisele whispered. "I am at the end of my strength."

The two men looked at each other over the head of the woman, both sick at what was happening in the world around them.

Krista carried her basket with bread and cheese into the shack. "This is no time for niceties." She cleared a space on an oil-stained surface, looking around for something to protect the food.

"Here!" Jan pulled a newspaper from his coat pocket.

Krista spread the newspaper out and began cutting slices from a fresh loaf of bread. She put the cheese on the newspaper. "I will heat some stew. The coffee is almost ready. The percolator will stay warm on the top of the fire to keep hot." She returned to the spirit stove she had set up on the floor of the garage.

Chapter 9

"I don't think I have ever tasted anything so wonderful." Gisele was dipping fresh bread into a bowl of stew.

"I have put a temporary wheel on your campervan." The mechanic appeared in the doorway of the shack. "You will drive it into the garage. The words on the side must be removed."

"What is wrong?" Jan demanded.

"That –" The mechanic looked at the women and bit back the curse on his lips. "Claus has been riding his bicycle past my gates."

"He is a known informer," Jan told them.

"I am going to drive to a garage that has the right tyres. I'll lock the gates leading to the road when I leave. You must be very careful. They know two Englishers are here. No one else must be seen to put their nose outside." The mechanic rubbed the bristles on his chin.

"When can we leave?" Perry looked at the worry on the faces of the two men.

"Not tonight – it is to happen here." The mechanic was visibly distraught.

He left with Krista on his heels. She would drive the van into the large garage.

Gisele wiped her bowl clean with a hunk of bread, content to sit and listen.

"What is to happen?" Perry asked.

"I had hoped that saner minds would prevail." Jan sighed. "There is a government-sanctioned order in place to remove Jews from our cities."

"Good God! Can we not warn them?" Perry asked.

"Do you not think we have tried! My country," he beat a clenched fist against his chest, "has become a world of fear. Neighbours are encouraged to spy on neighbour. Men and women disappear in the night, never to be seen again. We are being taught to hate."

"I am sorry." What else could Perry say? It would be hard for a man like Jan to stand and watch.

"I told you to leave." Jan turned to glare at Perry. "But in truth I am happy you have returned. I had no way to get Gisele out of Germany. The Jews too ignored my warnings. They insisted this is their home. They have families, businesses. Any people who help the Jews are being warned. They will be shot down in the streets as warning to others not to interfere." Jan had tried for months to encourage men he knew to flee with their families. His warnings had fallen on deaf ears – now it was too late.

"You can help no one if you are dead," Gisele said softly.

Krista appeared in the doorway. "I have moved the van. A man on his bike has cycled past at least twice."

"I need sleep." Gisele tried to stand. "I am of no use if I am exhausted."

"Come." Jan hurried to her side. "I will help you back to your pallet. You will be able to sleep while we keep watch."

Gisele accepted the help – she was at the end of her strength. "You should return to your home, Jan."

"I will not leave until I see you safely away," Jan objected.

"You are as stubborn as always." Gisele walked slowly out of the hut into the main body of the garage.

"Let's get the words off." Perry followed the others out of the hut.

"The hose is here." Krista wondered how Jan and Gisele knew each other.

Perry held the hose and directed the water while Krista used a long-handled brush to wash the words away.

"Thank goodness for waterproof material." Krista stood back, water beading on her clothing. "It was a blessing they used whitewash and not paint."

They returned the garage to order and stood for a moment, wondering what they should do.

"You two should try to sleep," Jan said. "I will keep watch."

"I don't think I could sleep." Krista's nerves were jangling.

"You must rest. If all goes well you will be driving through the early-morning hours towards the border," Jan insisted.

The tyres had been changed. Darkness had fallen. Jan and the mechanic, who had stayed to protect his buildings from whatever was to come, paced the length of the garage. Krista and Perry were lying down inside the campervan, each unable to sleep but trying to rest. Gisele, hadn't moved on her pallet.

"Come, you will bear witness." A hand slapped the outside of the van.

They pushed out of their sleeping bags and stepped from the van.

"Jan is in the trees." The mechanic, the hose in his hands, jerked his head towards the tall trees to the back of his property. "I must wet down my roof."

"Dear God!" Krista ran towards the trees. The night was on fire. Great clouds of flame and black smoke streaked towards the sky.

"It is the Jewish quarter." Jan's voice came from the shadows when the pair had reached the copse of trees.

"It is madness." Perry, the binoculars to his eyes, could see clearly what was happening below them. The flames lit the scene in colours of nightmare. "There are women and children down there." He passed the glasses to Krista.

The sound of screaming and smashing glass reached them even here on this out-of-the-way piece of land at the edge of Essen.

"The soldiers are shooting people!" Krista cried. "We must help them!"

Jan's large hands gripped her shoulders before she could move. "*What can you do for them but die with them?*" His voice was choked. "*We want you to bear witness to this madness. You must carry word to the world.*"

Perry wanted to weep. To be asked to stand here and witness something so horrible! "Man's inhumanity to man."

"I prayed that I had imagined it." Gisele appeared among the trees.

"*You should not be out!*" Jan barked. "*You must not be seen.*"

"You trained me to move softly and unseen." Jan had been the groundskeeper on her family's estate for many years.

"The soldiers are tearing children from their mother's arms!" Krista, the glasses to her eyes, cried.

"This is happening all over Germany." Jan kept his arm around Gisele's shaking shoulders as they stood, helpless at the horror taking place below them.

"*Englisher, help!*"

They turned to see burning missiles being lobbed over the locked gates onto the forecourt. Two men stood in the street, shouting abuse and laughing madly.

"*Jan, you cannot.*" Gisele held the man back with only her words.

Perry hurried to the mechanic's side. The hose was pushed into his hands. Krista, being more limber, was ordered to throw the contents of the red buckets filled with sand that stood along the side of the garage onto the flames.

The night seemed endless. The two throwing missiles into the garage appeared to hold a personal grudge against the mechanic. They ran off when they ran out of ammunition, perhaps to join the crowds gathered in the town.

The mechanic remained at his post, keeping watch over his business. Perry and Krista returned to join the others in the trees. They watched, each with their own thoughts as men were marched away while women and children were pushed towards trucks. The sounds and sights of that night would remain in their memory forever.

"It would be best if you left now," said Jan.

The frenzy of the crowd below was lessening. The soldiers were driving and leading the sobbing people away in the opposite direction to the one Krista would take. The sky was filled with black smoke. It was impossible to judge the time.

"You must not stop for anything you might see. You are carrying important cargo. It would not do for her to fall into the hands of the Nazis. I will ride my motorbike before you and lead the way. If we are stopped I will curse your blood and say I am removing you from German soil. I will be believed."

"*Jan, nooo!*" Gisele cried.

"I am an old man." He pressed a kiss to her forehead. "What is inside that head must not fall into Nazi hands." He hugged her close to his chest while she sobbed. "Come, the van is ready. You have petrol and everything else you could need. Do not stop for any reason. I will escort you towards the border. I will leave when we reach the forested area before it. God Speed." He pushed her from him and disappeared into the trees.

The mechanic crossed to the trees, shouting abuse and shaking his fist at them. He blamed them for the attack on his garage. He cursed them, telling them to get off his property. He shouted that he wanted money from them and then he never wanted to see them again. Krista didn't bother translating for Perry. It was all an act played out for anyone who might be watching.

The bill had been settled with traveller's cheques. Gisele was aboard the campervan and the mechanic was still shouting abuse while helping them in any way he could.

The sound of a heavy engine approaching the garage carried through the night. Jan, an official sash across his chest claiming his support of Hitler, stopped his heavy motorcycle outside the locked gates. He was coming to remove the Englishers, he shouted loudly over the engine noise. The mechanic hurried to open the gates, with much handwaving and shouted insults.

Krista drove the van out of the gates that slammed closed as soon as she had cleared them. She followed the lights of the bike back towards the main road. She kept her eyes fixed on that bright light, refusing to allow herself to see her surroundings. They had to leave. There was nothing they could do to help here. She could not think about what she had just seen. She would be a quivering wreck if she allowed herself to dwell on the horrors she had witnessed.

It was a silent journey along the main road in the direction of the Belgian border. The absence of the many guards they had passed along their route up to this point was very evident. The van travelled along unhindered. Perry groaned and covered his eyes from time to time but Krista didn't ask what had upset him.

She had a job to do. The road in front of her seemed never-ending.

They drove for hours, then the motorbike stopped and each vehicle used the cans they carried to refuel. They continued onwards as the sky lightened.

The motorbike rider tapped his brakes. The red taillight flickered.

"Gisele!" Perry turned his chair around. He walked to where Gisele slept on the floor. "Time to hide."

He helped the sleepy woman out of her sleeping bag and into the toilet. He removed the panel from one wall to reveal a hidden space big enough for two people to stand.

"God be with you!" Gisele whispered as Perry wrestled the panel back into place, concealing her. There were holes in the panel that matched those on the outside of the campervan. If asked, it was to allow the toilet odours to escape. They would provide air for her now.

Perry picked up the sleeping bag, stashing it in the space beneath the window seat. He checked that nothing was out of place.

Krista wished it had remained dark. Trucks carrying dead-eyed women and children passed them on the road. Soldiers ignored them, calling back and forth to each other. They high-stepped along, seeming to celebrate their night's activities.

"They must be heading for the train station," Perry remarked.

Some time passed.

"Jan is leaving us," Perry said.

They watched the motorbike pull to the side of the road. Jan shook his fist as they passed him.

"Do not stop for any reason, Krista," Perry said as they entered an area shaded by trees. "People will be desperate to escape this place. We cannot help them. It will be difficult to do but we must escape. We have much to report and cannot afford to endanger this mission." He was speaking to convince himself as much as Krista.

"I want to keep driving until I fall off the edge of the world." Krista had been fighting tears for what seemed like forever. "It will be very difficult to pretend to be a silly woman on her way home."

"I know but needs must ..."

They sat in silence as the guard on the German side of the border demanded their papers. There was no demand to search the campervan as there had been when they entered the country. The guards seemed subdued and nervous. They were waved through towards Belgium.

"We need to find an out-of-the-way place to park, Krista," Perry said as they crossed the space between one country and another. "I want to let Gisele out of the hidey-hole as soon as we can."

"The Belgian side of the forest we camped in our first night in Germany is just over the border. We can stop there."

Chapter 10

"This is such a clever little vehicle."

Gisele, zipped into a sleeping bag, was sitting on the floor of the campervan, her back to the wall. They had been waved through the Belgian border control. The campervan was parked inside a dense copse of trees. Perry was outside, fetching wood for the fire. Krista was lying on the bench under the window, a sleeping bag covering her.

"What did Jan mean?" Krista pushed onto an elbow to look at the other woman.

"I beg your pardon?"

"Jan – he said what was inside your head could not fall into German hands." Krista wanted an answer. They had risked their lives for this woman. "What did he mean?"

"Ah, dear Jan!" Gisele pulled the old-fashioned hat from her head. "What would I have done without him?" She ran her hands through her dirty hair.

"It is freezing out there." Perry threw an armful of kindling into the van. "I'll soon have the fire going." He stepped into the uneasy silence in the van.

"Gisele is about to explain Jan's strange remarks to me." Krista didn't feel she needed to explain.

"Women!" Perry turned his attention to getting the fire going. They were all cold and tired.

"I met my husband at University." Gisele pulled the hat back on. She leaned her head against the wall and closed her eyes. "He was my professor. I fell in love with his mind." Tears rolled slowly down her ashen cheeks. "Science fascinates me – it always has. My husband encouraged me to explore the possibilities of gases." She opened her eyes to find them both staring at her. "I will not bore you with the details but it would appear I am something of a prodigy. I did not want fame or fortune. It is the science that fascinates me. My husband used my research to publish many papers in renowned scientific journals. He became somewhat of a celebrity in the world of science. My name appears nowhere on his papers."

"Oh, oh!" Krista sat up. "*You* are the scientist!"

Perry, the fire going, took the seat beside her. She threw part of the sleeping bag over his lap.

"Indeed," Gisele sobbed. "I gave him the life he wanted. A family and fame. He gave me encouragement and a place to work and develop my ideas. The Nazis thought to use the wife and children of Herr Professor to encourage him to develop his deadly gases."

What could anyone say? They rested quietly while the fire warmed the air in the van.

"I'll make a pot of coffee. We should have something to eat before we get back on the road." Krista busied herself in the kitchen space. "Those clothes cannot possibly be yours." Krista gestured at the old-fashioned black suit. Gisele looked like a wizened old lady. She could not be that old. She was Captain Waters' twin after all.

"Do you know how it feels to owe your life and freedom to a pigeon!" Gisele laughed bitterly. "I don't know what made me check the pigeon coop on the roof of our apartment building. I had packed for the children the night before and stored their little cases in my car. I never told my husband the children were to be taken to England." How could you explain the fear and mistrust she had been living with? "Their nanny was a paid-up member of the Nazi party and proud of it. "I received my brother's warning. I had time only to tell him I would flee. I released all of the pigeons. The children's nanny had left a box of donations for her church in the apartment hallway. I grabbed the darkest oldest ugliest outfit I could find and stuffed it into a shopping bag. I don't think I took a breath until I had seen the children on their way."

"Do you have papers?" Perry wasn't interested in the woman's outfit. They had to get her out of the country. He needed to know if they had to smuggle her. She could be injured if she had to remain in the campervan while it was hoisted onto the deck of the ferry. If she had official papers she could openly travel with them.

"Jan destroyed the false papers I travelled with to reach Essen." Gisele climbed out of the sleeping bag. "I have my British passport under my own name. It is, believe it or not, under my hat."

Perry took the sleeping bag she offered him and stood to stuff the bags back under the seat. It didn't take the campervan long to warm up.

"There were German soldiers on the docks when last I sailed from Antwerp." Krista opened the legs of the table. She doubted any of them wanted to eat but they must keep up their strength. "They appeared free to question travellers while officials looked away."

"We will need a story to tell if and when we are stopped." Perry raised a brow when Krista started to laugh.

"It would seem old Brunhilda Alvensleben will once more come to the rescue." Krista had not thought she'd be capable of laughter.

"Explain?" Gisele knew she had missed something.

"Your brother sent us into Germany with an urn ..."

The three made themselves comfortable while Perry and Krista regaled a fascinated Gisele with the tale of Brunhilda.

"And this means what?" Gisele had enjoyed their story. It had distracted them all long enough to force food down.

"Don't you see?" Krista's eyes sparkled. "You are already dressed like an elderly widow. If I push you in the wheelchair – sobbing as if your heart is broken – along the dock – no one would question you. Men, even soldiers, don't like dealing with crying women!" She stood with her hands on her hips, grinning widely.

"The urn is nearly empty." Perry had intended to bury the urn before they left this camp site.

"There are ashes in the fireplace," Krista replied.

The sound of three people laughing hysterically echoed from the campsite. When one got control of their laughter, they would look at another and start again. It was the release of tension they all so desperately needed.

The journey through Antwerp was anti-climactic. The people of Antwerp had enough of their own problems. They paid scant attention to a sobbing figure in a wheelchair being pushed along the cobbled streets. They visited the ferry office to purchase tickets. While there Perry and Gisele used the ferry company's telegraph operator to send telegrams to England. The book of traveller's cheques was a great deal thinner than when they had left home.

Krista felt she had no one who needed to be notified.

German soldiers were once more present on the docks. They paid no attention to two sobbing women, one in a wheelchair with a large urn on her lap and a limping man. Their papers were given a cursory inspection – only their tickets were closely checked. The campervan attracted attention because it was unusual and gave people something to look at and wonder about. It was hoisted onto the deck of the ferry with no problem. There was no need to present the urn, now holding fireplace ashes.

"I feel as if I won't be able to breathe freely until the ferry has docked in Felixstowe." Gisele was glad she was seated. She was trembling visibly. She had done it

– with a great deal of help – she had escaped Hitler's clutches. She could not dwell on her husband. He was a charming man. She was sure he could talk himself out of his troubles.

"I think it is time to give Brunhilda Alvensleben a decent send-off." Krista took the urn from Gisele's lap before she let it fall. "A burial at sea should be just the thing."

"Do you need me to come with you?" Perry felt possessive of the old girl – no matter how fictional.

"I'll wait until we are out to sea." Krista would enjoy some time alone to think.

"Goodbye, Brunhilda!" Krista stood at the stern of the ferry and opened her hands, allowing the urn to slip over the side and into the foaming sea. Gisele and Perry were snuggled down under blankets, trying to sleep in chairs bolted into the deck of the traveller's lounge. "I have enjoyed having your company. I will miss you." She didn't feel silly. The urn had been almost a third person on this journey. "You were the first and last relative I've ever known." She had tears slipping down her cheeks. She didn't try to wipe them away. She needed to cry.

She looked out over the grey sea, her heart heavy. She had been here only six months ago. So much had happened. She had met people who offered her help. She had learned the secrets of her own past. But what was she to do now? She looked at the sky, tears running freely down her upraised face. She stood looking to the sky for a long time as if subconsciously waiting for a reply to her worries from the heavens.

"There you are!" Perry's voice drew her from her melancholy. "I've been looking for you."

"I was saying goodbye to Brunhilda." She wiped her cheeks before turning to face him.

"She was a great old girl." Perry joined her at the railing.

They stood watching the sea for a while enjoying this break from the constant stress they had been under since they started out on this journey.

"I am hoping my father will meet me when we arrive at Felixstowe." Perry was still looking at the sea. "I need to tell him of all of the submarines available to the German navy. There is much we need to discuss." When she said nothing, he turned to look down at her bent head. "Gisele believes her twin Captain Waters will be waiting on the dock. They have not seen each other for some time."

When she didn't look at him or say anything, he sought for something to say. He had never been uncomfortable in her company before.

"My father can give you a lift to the nearest train station if that is your wish. You must be eager to return home. I know I am."

Krista raised her eyes to look at him. This wonderful kind man she had thought would be important in her life. The time they had spent together had been fraught with danger. She had never felt so close to anyone. She wanted to sigh. He was more a brother to her than the three men she had believed to be her brothers. She thought about his words. Did she need a lift to a train station? To go where? Where was home to her now?

"I will offer to drive the campervan for Captain

Waters." The time alone in the van would give her time to think. "But, thank you, Perry, for everything."

They stood watching the shores of England approach, each wondering what the future held. Not only for them but the world as they knew it.

THE END

Made in the USA
Middletown, DE
14 September 2020

19591951R00062